THE SECRET OF THE REALMS

AN EXTENDED NOVELIZATION

FOR GABE, MATTHEW,
AND LUKE
–MR

FOR MY WIFE, KRISTI
–TF

Printed in the United States of America
First Hardcover Edition, September 2018

1 3 5 7 9 10 8 6 4 2

FAC-020093-18242

Library of Congress Control Number: 2018930677

ISBN 978-1-368-02035-0

Designed by Gegham Vardanyan

disneybooks.com

SUSTAINABLE Certified Sourcing
FORESTRY
INITIATIVE www.sfiprogram.org
SFI-00993

THIS LABEL APPLIES TO TEXT STOCK

DISNEY
THE
NUTCRACKER
AND THE
FOUR REALMS

THE SECRET OF THE REALMS
AN EXTENDED NOVELIZATION

BY MEREDITH RUSU
ART BY THOMAS FLUHARTY
SCREEN STORY BY ASHLEIGH POWELL
SCREENPLAY BY ASHLEIGH POWELL AND TOM MCCARTHY
SUGGESTED BY THE SHORT STORY
"THE NUTCRACKER AND THE MOUSE KING" WRITTEN BY E.T.A. HOFFMAN,
AND THE "NUTCRACKER BALLET" WRITTEN BY MARIUS PETIPA

DISNEY PRESS
LOS ANGELES • NEW YORK

CHAPTER 1

CLARA

Pine cones. Cinnamon. Roasted chestnuts and crackling firewood. The scents mingled in the air, rising high and swirling with wisps of chimney smoke and snow flurries. For a moment, they wafted just below the gathering snow clouds, seeming to form their own billowy puff of Christmastime spirit. Then, with a *thwoop*, the scents, smoke, and snow all scattered against the mighty beat of an owl's wings.

The owl swooped down from the clouds toward the city below. If it noticed the scents drifting up from the cobblestoned streets, it didn't show it. Rather, the owl flew along its path resolute and strong, dipping lower and flying so swiftly that its shadow seemed to skate across the snow-iced rooftops. Smoke puffed out from chimney stacks upon the rows and rows of buildings. The frozen river Thames danced with children ice-skating in the distance. And as the sun sank below the horizon, lamplighters used long poles to kindle streetlamps so storefronts and trinket peddlers were cast aglow in soft, warm light.

Candles flickered in windows. Shop owners adjusted ribbons on door wreaths. Men and women bundled their cloaks more tightly as they bustled this way and that, carrying presents and herding rosy-cheeked children toward home. Then, faintly in the distance, a church bell chimed, signaling the start of the most magical evening of all.

Christmas Eve, London.

Now, the owl wasn't much concerned with the hustle and bustle. It had eyes for only one thing: an evening snack.

There! It spotted its target—a tiny mouse scurrying along an attic window ledge. Father Christmas might be arriving that evening expecting cookies, but the owl thought a furry treat was just the thing.

The owl flew closer. Its shadow fell across the mouse. The owl swooped. . . .

It missed!

In the nick of time, the mouse darted through a hole in the brick masonry beside the window and disappeared. The owl hooted in dismay. It landed on the window ledge and waited. It blinked. But the mouse didn't reemerge. After a long while, the owl hooted again and glided away, keeping its eyes peeled for another tasty morsel.

Inside the brick wall, the mouse scurried along a narrow tunnel just wide enough for a mouse to fit through. It was in search of its own tasty morsel. And in the dusty attics and shadowed cellars of London, while happy families were making merry and paying little attention to the nooks and crannies about them, there was always something worth scavenging just before dark.

The tunnel widened and a dim light shone at the end. The mouse burst out into a large attic room.

Squeak! There! Sitting in the center of the room was a scrumptious-looking biscuit. Why a freshly baked treat would be resting in its own little cleared space on the grimy floor of a cluttered attic, or how it had gotten there, weren't thoughts that crossed the mouse's mind. All it knew was that there was a delicious dinner a few feet away, and it wasn't going to let it slip through its paws.

As the mouse inched up to the biscuit, it never noticed the curious eyes watching it from the shadows. Eyes that were far keener and far craftier than the owl's.

"You really want to catch that mouse, Fritz?" Clara Stahlbaum whispered to her little brother. With her tangled hair and mussed dress, she was all but invisible in the corner. But her clever brown eyes shone.

"Yes!" Fritz insisted eagerly.

Clara smiled. Catching the mouse they'd heard scurrying about the attic at night was the only thing little Fritz had talked about—since three o'clock that afternoon.

She struck a match, illuminating both their faces. "Then this is how you do it," she said confidently. "With science, mechanics, and a little bit of luck."

She carefully lit a tea light candle. Playing with fire anywhere in the house—especially the attic—was strictly forbidden. But this wasn't playing. This was science, and she knew what she was doing.

Clara gingerly moved the candle under a miniature hot-air balloon—the first component of her brilliant contraption. Spread around the attic was a series of levers, pulleys, and ramps activated by balloons, balls, and toys, all positioned with precise calculation. And at the end of her invention was a basket, ready to drop over the unsuspecting mouse as soon as it nibbled the biscuit.

It was perfect. All her invention needed was the right touch to get it going.

"First, we've got energy," she whispered to Fritz. "The heat from the candle makes the balloon rise."

Fritz watched in wonder as the balloon rose and bumped into a ball waiting at the top of a wooden ramp.

"We get momentum from the ball," Clara explained.

Tap. The ball knocked into a toy monkey.

"Which hits the monkey, who pivots onto the bellows."

"Which blows the longboat." Fritz could barely contain his excitement as a fireplace bellows began to puff out air, pushing along a toy boat on wheels.

"Giving us Newton's third law of physics," Clara finished. "For every action, there is an equal and opposite reaction. And with a little bit of luck . . ."

Thwack! The longboat knocked into the basket, toppling it right over the mouse, biscuit and all!

"Mousetrap!" Fritz clapped his hands.

Clara beamed with pride as she and Fritz walked over to examine the tiny mouse captured beneath the basket. Her invention had been a stellar success, if she did say so herself.

"Fantastic," she whispered. "I can't wait to show—"

Clara stopped speaking abruptly. Luckily, Fritz was so pre-occupied with his furry new captive that he didn't notice. Didn't notice the pale ghost of sadness that crossed Clara's face, nor the hint of the word that hadn't yet crossed her lips.

"Mother," Clara finished to herself softly.

It had been just a few short months since the children's mother, Marie, had passed away. The pain of loss was bitterly fresh, especially for fourteen-year-old Clara. She had been incredibly close to her mother. Marie's absence was still new enough that, at times, Clara would forget herself and call out for her from another room, or would anticipate showing her a new invention like the one she'd made now, only to realize she could not.

Of all the Stahlbaum children—Louise, the eldest; Clara, the middle child; and Fritz, their energetic younger brother—Clara had been the one to truly follow in their mother's footsteps. Marie had been an accomplished inventor, a tinkerer, as their family lovingly called it. And while Louise had inherited their mother's grace and poise, and Fritz her love of laughter, Clara alone had inherited her knack for inventing. Wheels and cogs, pistons and pulleys, levels and counterweights and gears—it all made sense to Clara. Like tiny pieces of the world that she could hold and manipulate and build to do great things. But her mother had been the real genius. She was able to make even the tiniest, most intricate contraptions come to life. Over the years, she had taught Clara everything she knew. Patiently. Lovingly. Piece by piece, gear by gear.

One of Clara's greatest joys had been completing a new invention and seeing the look of pride on her mother's face when it worked properly the very first time. But now, though the knowledge and tools remained, Clara couldn't help feeling that the joy—the spark that brought it all to life—had faded along with her mother.

"Do you think Father will let me keep him?" Fritz asked anxiously, still completely absorbed in the little mouse. "As a pet?"

Clara gave a half smile. Their father would most definitely *not* allow Fritz to keep the furry rodent as a family pet. But seeing her little brother so happy, and knowing that at least her invention had brought him excitement on this holiday that would feel so different this year, Clara didn't have the heart to tell him no.

Suddenly, the trapdoor in the attic floor flew open, knocking the basket askew and freeing the mouse. The tiny critter squeaked and scampered off, darting beneath a crate and back through a hole in the attic wall.

"*Oh!*" Fritz groaned in dismay. "We nearly had him! Can we try again? Can we?"

Before Clara could answer, a head popped up through the trapdoor. It was Mrs. Ashmore, the family cook.

"There you are!" the portly cook huffed. "Up and down I've been looking for you rascals. Worn out, I am."

The cook sniffed the air. Thinking fast, Clara whisked the matches behind her back and out of sight. She watched nervously as the cook passed an eye around the attic, checking for signs of mischief.

"We were just catching a mouse," Fritz explained.

The cook wiped her brow. "Well, I didn't bake your favorite biscuits to have them sitting lonely on the parlor table."

"Ginger biscuits?" Fritz asked in delight.

"Yes, Master Fritz." Mrs. Ashmore nodded. "Ginger biscuits. Quick, now. We have a lot to do before this evening."

Clara and Fritz clamored down the attic ladder and into the hallway. They descended a long staircase, where their older sister, Louise, was waiting for them.

"Look at the state of you," Louise scolded. She wiped a large smudge of dirt from Fritz's trousers.

"We were in the attic!" Fritz exclaimed. "Trying to catch a mouse with toys and momentum and matches—"

"Matches?" Louise asked sharply.

Clara sucked in her breath.

"It was Clara's idea," Fritz said quickly.

Clara shot Fritz a look while Louise's face grew stern.

"Clara Stahlbaum, you *know* the dangers of matches in the house, especially the attic," Louise scolded.

Clara didn't answer. *Of course* she knew the danger of matches. But she wasn't a novice—she was a tinkerer. And she always took proper safety measures when using dangerous tools for her contraptions. Like matches. Or knives. Sometimes a saw (which, her mother had promised, would remain a secret between them).

But for some reason, Louise thought of Clara's handiwork as child's play, when really, it was so much more.

Admittedly, Clara had the habit of getting into predicaments. Sometimes her complex contraptions would take over entire rooms of the house. Or her tinkering tools would accidentally get left in places where people might step or sit on them. Without fail, Louise would point out the grease streaking Clara's hair and the oil staining her dress *just* before the family was supposed to go somewhere important. It was in those moments that Louise would insist it was mad for a young lady like Clara to spend so much time tinkering.

But Mother never made me feel ashamed, Clara thought. Instead, her mother had always smiled and gently helped Clara clean the grime from her hair, and had been patient when a room was off-limits because of an invention in progress. Her mother understood her the way no one else could. Being scolded by Louise like a little child playing recklessly, when her tinkering was anything *but* playing, stung.

"No harm done," Mrs. Ashmore interceded for them. "I made sure of that."

Louise frowned. "They shouldn't have been up there in the first place. Come. Father is waiting for us in the parlor."

With a whoop, Fritz bounded down the hall. Clara and Louise followed behind, a bit more decorously. Clara cast a sideways glance at Louise. Her older sister didn't seem truly cross. She looked more preoccupied than anything. Clara's resentment softened. She figured she knew what was on Louise's mind: what Christmas surprise did their father have waiting for them just a few rooms away?

Their mother had always had a way of bringing the family parlor to life like a Christmastime forest. She'd hang fresh pine garlands from the mantel and tables, and arrange shiny red ornaments upon the tree branches so that they twinkled like glowing fireflies. "It's like a picture from a storybook!" Clara would always exclaim. Her mother would smooth Clara's hair, kiss her head, and say, "Yes, my darling. It's imagination brought to life."

This year, Clara hadn't even been sure they would decorate for Christmas. They had only just removed the mourning wreath from their door, and black lace still covered her mother's vanity mirror. But their father had promised to take care of everything: to put up the tree, hang the stockings, and even drape the garlands just as their mother had. He had promised his children that Christmas would still be magical, because that was something their mother had wanted very, very much.

And in her heart of hearts, Clara hoped that, somehow, her father was right.

Fritz raced up to the parlor doors and burst through. Clara and Louise followed.

"Well, well!" Charles Stahlbaum greeted his children from where he was perched precariously on a chair, positioning the star at the top of the tree. "What about this?"

He hopped down and gestured to the tree with a flourish.

Clara and her siblings stopped. They stared.

It . . . wasn't what Clara had been expecting.

Garlands and ribbons were draped about the room, but rather thinly, not at all like a wintertime forest. A wreath hung slightly askew upon the mantel beneath a portrait of the children's late mother. The lopsided tree tilted a bit too far to the left. The ornaments hung a bit haphazardly. Clara could tell her father had tried hard. But it was all just a bit . . . off.

"It's—wonderful, Father!" Louise forced a smile.

Mr. Stahlbaum looked ruefully back to the tree. "Well, with a few adjustments . . ."

"That's not how Mother did it," Fritz blurted out.

Clara shushed Fritz. But it was too late. Mr. Stahlbaum's shoulders slumped. They all knew Fritz was right.

"Well," Mr. Stahlbaum said huskily. He tried to give a small laugh. "Come help me then, Fritz."

The children gathered around the tree and helped their father adjust the delicate ornaments along the branches. Louise stepped up on the chair to straighten the star, and Clara fixed the ribbons and garlands about the room. Soon the parlor looked at least more presentable, if not perfect.

"Now, children." Mr. Stahlbaum clasped his hands. "I have some presents."

"Presents!" Fritz cheered.

"But it's not Christmas Day." Louise cocked her head.

Clara watched curiously as her father picked up three beautifully wrapped boxes from under the tree. Was this their father's way of trying to make the evening merry?

"They're special presents," Mr. Stahlbaum said slowly. "From your mother."

Silence.

"Your mother wanted to—she wanted you to have something special to remember her by." Mr. Stahlbaum was struggling to find the words. "And she asked me to give them to you on Christmas Eve."

The children hesitantly took hold of their presents. Clara felt a rush of emotion with the weight of the gift in her hands. *Did Mother wrap this herself?* she wondered. *Did she hold this in her hands, knowing I would, too, after she was gone?*

Fritz opened his present first. He tore off the paper, revealing ten toy tin soldiers. The sadness of the moment flitted away from his expression, replaced with giggles of delight. These were just the tin soldiers he'd shown his mother in the toy-store window! He lined them up, preparing them for battle.

Next was Louise. She sat gracefully upon the sofa and opened her gift box. When she saw what was inside, she gasped.

"What is it?" Clara asked.

"It's Mother's favorite," Louise replied, pulling out a soft green gown edged in delicate lace.

Clara's eyes grew wide. It was the dress their mother had worn last Christmas. Her gaze drifted as the memory flooded back—how she'd clamored into the parlor along with Fritz, carrying baskets of decorations. They'd found their mother waiting for them beside the tree, dressed in the beautiful gown. Elegant and regal, like a queen.

"So it is," Mr. Stahlbaum told Louise.

"But I can't, can I?" Louise asked.

"You can," their father assured her. "She very much wanted you to."

Louise stood and held the lovely gown against her body. "Oh, it's beautiful! Shall I wear it to the party?"

Clara felt a tightness in her chest. *The party.* Just hearing it mentioned made it feel all the more real: in just a short while, they would be headed to Godfather Drosselmeyer's house for his annual Christmas ball.

"I think that's exactly what it's for," Mr. Stahlbaum told Louise.

Clara sighed. *I wish we didn't have to go,* she thought.

Normally, Clara looked forward to this particular party all year long. After all, the celebration was something her mother and godfather had invented together, back when Marie was just a young girl being raised by Drosselmeyer on his estate.

In fact, Drosselmeyer was a world-renowned inventor, and not just of celebrations. He was an inventor of all sorts of things, big and small. Horseless carriages, mechanized toys, even flying apparatuses—his entire estate was a menagerie of mechanical wonders, all carefully crafted by him and his protégé, Marie. He had taught Marie everything she knew about tinkering, and in turn, they had both taught Clara. Clara had spent many, many happy hours with her mother and Godfather Drosselmeyer, learning the tricks of the trade in his fabulous workshop.

But the Christmas party was the most special time of all. It was the one night a year when hundreds of guests were welcomed into his majestic ballroom to marvel at his collection and delight in holiday revelry—a night filled with wonder and cheer and even a little magic. It had been the celebration Clara loved most to share with her family, especially her mother.

But without Mother, how can it be the same? Clara thought.

She swallowed and put on a brave face. Everyone was trying so hard to make tonight special. Her father was trying. Louise was trying. Even Fritz still seemed to be holding on to an invisible golden thread of holiday magic that kept the entire evening from unraveling. Clara had to try, too. For them.

She nervously turned her gift over in her hands. This was it. The final treasure her mother could ever give her.

"Go on, Clara," her father encouraged. "It's okay."

Holding her breath, Clara peeled away the paper. The wrapping fell apart easily and fluttered to the chair. And inside was . . . was . . .

"An egg?" Clara asked, bewildered.

Her gift was an ornate metal egg. Intricate patterns of spirals and flourishes were etched into the casing. And a seam wrapped around the middle, sealed shut with a six-pointed star lock.

"Isn't that pretty, Clara?" Louise asked.

Clara wasn't quite sure what to make of it. The egg was beautiful, yes. But she couldn't help feeling disappointed that it wasn't something . . . more. Not more valuable. But more meaningful. For a fleeting moment, she'd hoped that her mother's final gift would be a message or a memory or even a recording of her voice—perhaps something they had been working on together before Marie had grown ill. The egg-shaped box was lovely. But it didn't feel right.

"It's—yes, it's beautiful," Clara said finally. She tried to open it. "But it's locked."

"There's probably a key somewhere," Louise offered. She rummaged through the wrapping paper. As she did so, a sealed note fluttered to the floor. It was addressed to Clara, in her mother's handwriting.

Clara quickly took hold of the envelope and opened it.

To my beautiful Clara, it read. *All I can give you is here. Everything you need is inside.*

Clara's heart leaped. Her mother *had* left her something more. The note said so itself—everything she needed was inside the trinket box! What could possibly be so valuable, so meaningful, that it was all her mother could give her—yet it fit inside a tiny, perfect egg?

There was only one way to find out.

Clara peeled out of the room.

"Clara?" her father called after her in concern.

But Clara didn't stop. She ran straight to the staircase and up the stairs, turned the landing, and ran up a second flight.

She ran, ran, ran all the way up to her parents' bedroom, making a beeline for her mother's vanity table. She pulled open the dresser drawer and began searching through her mother's tinkering tools, careful not to disturb the black lace shroud covering the vanity mirror.

She was so focused she ignored the soft knock on the open bedroom door behind her.

"Clara?" her father asked gently.

"I am searching for the key," Clara said without looking up.

But as she rummaged deeper in the drawer without success, Clara grew frustrated. The key wasn't there. Her mother *always* kept important things in this drawer. It was where all their shared tinkering tools were stored. The key *should* be there. So why wasn't it?

Clara grabbed some of the tools instead and sat upon the bed. She began forcing them one by one into the egg's keyhole. But the stubborn lock refused to budge.

"Nothing?" her father asked.

Clara shook her head. Tears prickled at the corners of her eyes. She brushed a hand across her face and kept trying. Needle-nose pliers. A tiny screwdriver. Fine-point tweezers. Nothing worked.

"Papa," Clara asked, discouraged, "why would Mother give me a box without a key?"

"I don't know," he replied. "I'm sure there was a very good reason she wanted you to have it."

"I have to see what is inside," Clara insisted. "I have to."

Whatever was in there, whatever treasure her mother had tucked away inside that tiny, precious egg, was a last wisp connecting Clara to the one person she missed more than anything. The last thing her mother could ever give her. Whatever was inside was everything to Clara.

Her father sat on the bed next to her. "May I?" He reached for the note addressed to Clara and read it. "Oh, I see. Oh, dear. And none of your tools work?"

Clara shook her head. "It's a pin tumbler lock."

"And that's bad, is it, my little mechanic?" Mr. Stahlbaum asked with a knowing smile.

"Very." Clara nodded. She couldn't hold back her tears any longer. "What's the point of Christmas without her, Papa?"

Mr. Stahlbaum wrapped his arm around her shoulders. "I know this is hard, my dear. I know."

Just then, Louise appeared in the doorway dressed in Marie's beautiful gown.

"Oh!" Mr. Stahlbaum exclaimed.

Clara gave a start. If she hadn't known any better, she would have sworn a young version of her mother was standing in the doorway. The dress suited Louise perfectly, tapering just right at her sister's slender waist and gracing her arms with its delicate lace-edged sleeves.

"Oh, my dear," Mr. Stahlbaum breathed. "You look just as lovely as your mother."

"You really think so, Papa?" Louise asked, filled with hope. She turned to Clara. "Do you think so, too?"

Clara wiped her eyes. She didn't want Louise to see she had been crying. "I do," she agreed. "Mother was right to leave it to you. You look perfect. Everyone will think so."

Louise caught the remnants of tears upon Clara's cheeks. She swept in to hug her little sister. "And you will look perfect, too," she insisted. "I will tidy you up for Drosselmeyer's Christmas party, and we will both look as lovely as Mother would have wanted us to."

Clara hugged her sister back. But inside, she felt like she was falling apart.

The egg shifted, its weight heavy in her lap. Clara glanced down. There was still the chance to hear one final message from her mother, if she could just unlock the egg. She had to hold on to that hope.

She needed to find the key.

"Come," Louise told Clara comfortingly. "We shall find you a beautiful dress, run a brush through your hair, and pick out your best pair of shoes. We have a party to attend."

CHAPTER 2

CLARA

A short while later, Clara and her family clip-clopped along London's cobblestoned streets in a horse-drawn carriage. Clara watched flurries collect on the ledge of the carriage window. They passed a group of carolers serenading a mother and little girl on their doorstep. No one else would have paid attention, but Clara took note of how the mother lovingly stroked her daughter's hair.

Clara sighed and turned her attention back to the trinket box resting in her lap. Though the carriage jostled, the billowy ruffles of her lavender party dress kept the delicate treasure in place. Louise had selected one of her finest gowns for Clara to borrow for Drosselmeyer's party. She'd brushed and pinned Clara's hair to perfection, too. Clara patted the side of her head. Her hair felt different from how her mother used to do it—pinned a little too tightly. And her feet were uncomfortable in the high-heeled shoes Louise had insisted she wear. When her mother used to help her dress for Drosselmeyer's party, she'd always somehow managed to brush the forest of tangles from Clara's hair with the softest touch. And she'd secretly allow Clara to wear a well-worn pair of party slippers so her feet wouldn't blister. Clara would ask her mother if she looked beautiful, and her mother would answer, *Of course, my clever darling. You are beautiful inside and out, as only you can be.* Clara so missed the reassuring comfort of her mother's hands. Delicate but steady, the way a tinkerer's should be.

Now, instead, Clara took comfort in the weight of the tool pouch she'd surreptitiously brought along. She withdrew one of her fine tweezers and began poking at the trinket box lock again.

"Clara, you're bringing tools to a party?" Louise spotted her immediately.

"I need to unlock this," Clara replied, maneuvering a tweezer point into the tiny keyhole. Nope. Still nothing. She turned the delicate egg over in her hands and held it up to the passing lamplight for a closer look. That was when she noticed the letter *D* engraved in calligraphy on the base.

"Drosselmeyer! That's his signature!" Clara drew in a sharp breath. If her godfather had created this, then surely he had the key to unlock it!

"Here we are," Louise suddenly announced.

All three children poked their heads out through the carriage windows to see the grand sight that was Drosselmeyer's stately manor, decorated in all its Christmastime majesty.

The mansion's steeple-roofed towers were draped with lush garlands, looping from balconies to buttresses. Every window was awash with the warm glow of light from within, and red and gold Chinese lanterns illuminated the path to the ornate wrought-iron gates inscribed with Drosselmeyer's signature letter D. By now the snow had stopped, leaving bushes and brambles frosted with shimmering ice crystals. It was like a scene from a fairy tale. Clara thought it was no wonder her mother had such a vivid imagination, growing up in a place like this. As she liked to do every year, Clara looked up to observe the nearly dozen chimney stacks lining the rooftops. Each puffed away with smoke—a sign that the heart of the house was beating, like a trusted, industrious machine.

The carriage rolled to a stop in front of the gates. There were no servants standing duty. Instead, the gates began to open on their own.

"Look at the gate!" Fritz cried in amazement. "How does it know we're here?"

"Pneumatics," Clara told him.

"Neu-whatics?" Fritz asked.

Clara leaned over next to Fritz and pointed out the window. "You see that machine back there? It's connected to the mechanical arms, which control the gate hinges. The weight of the carriage on the pad in front of the gate activates the mechanism."

Fritz's eyes glowed in wonder. "Magic!" he breathed.

"Honestly, Clara, where do you pick these things up?" Louise asked as the family stepped down from the carriage.

Clara was about to reply cheekily that she'd *learned* it from one of Drosselmeyer's books. But luckily, all talk of pneumatics floated away the moment they entered the house.

Drosselmeyer's estate décor could only be described with one word: eclectic. Vibrant red walls were lined with gold-leaf accents and treasures from her godfather's travels all over the world: Indian tapestries, African pottery, Chinese drapes. Jade dragons snaked along display alcoves and ancient scrolls sat rolled up in decoratively painted desks and cubbies. Even the entrance to his estate was a veritable museum of continental art and oddities, which for the Christmas season had been adorned with customary boughs of holly and red-ribbon wreaths. It was a mixture of global riches and Christmas finery that mesmerized all who saw it.

Servants took Clara's and her family's coats and promptly hung them on hooks connected to a conveyor belt. The mechanism whizzed the coats off to another room deep within the manor.

"Whoa," Fritz breathed.

White-gloved footmen stood at the doors to the great hall announcing families as they entered. Many of the party guests had already arrived. The ballroom was alive with people mingling and dancing in their Christmas finery, sipping on port and making merry. Servants passed by carrying gold platters of pastries and champagne. Children laughed as a mechanical sleigh piled high with presents appeared to take flight thanks to eight mechanized reindeer. And at the center of the room stood a towering Christmas tree bedecked in blazing red and gold. It was the only source of light for the entire hall, but it shone brighter than any chandelier ever could with a thousand tiny gaslights.

"Incredible," Mr. Stahlbaum murmured. "Drosselmeyer never fails to outdo himself."

"Do you see him?" Clara whispered to Fritz, scanning the crowd.

"Drosselmeyer?" Fritz asked. "No. Wait—is that him?"

He pointed to a tall man with a shock of frizzled gray hair who was quickly disappearing among the throngs of guests.

"You're right," Clara said.

With that, she slipped away from her family, ducking past the footmen and in among the tightly packed people. She faintly heard her family member's names announced, including hers, but she didn't have time for introductions. She was on a mission. From her mother.

A few partygoers cast her disapproving looks when she accidentally stepped on their toes before she finally caught up with the gray-haired man.

"Godfather?" she asked, touching him on the sleeve.

The man turned, and Clara's face fell. It was a ruddy-faced guest wearing an ill-fitting hairpiece that, in the candlelight, resembled Drosselmeyer's hair. It was not her godfather after all.

"Oh, I beg your pardon," she said. The man looked at her quizzically before walking away.

Clara sighed. It wasn't like her godfather to be away from

the celebration. He was always a gracious host, regaling guests with fascinating stories from his travels abroad. Where could he be?

She was about to resume her search when, suddenly, someone spoke behind her.

"May I have this dance?"

Clara turned. It was her father, his hand outstretched.

"Oh, I'm a terrible dancer, Papa," Clara insisted. She was being truthful. Clara loved music, but she always seemed to trip over her own two feet during a waltz.

"So am I!" Mr. Stahlbaum grinned. "We'll make the perfect couple."

Still, Clara hesitated.

"Please?" Mr. Stahlbaum asked, hopeful. "Just one. It's Christmas."

Clara gave in and nodded. She took her father's hand, and he led her to the dance floor. But the moment the string quartet started up the next waltz, Clara felt a tightness in her chest again. The tune was much, much too familiar, haunting and beautiful and more than she could bear.

Her mother's favorite song.

And just like that, Clara didn't want to be at the party

anymore. Everyone was acting like nothing had happened. But something *had* happened. Her mother was gone. How could they still celebrate without her?

Clara turned and raced up the nearest staircase.

"Clara, my dear, wait—" Mr. Stahlbaum pleaded.

But Clara didn't stop. She needed now, more than ever, to know what her mother had left for her inside the trinket box.

She swept past women's ruffled skirts and brushed against men's wool suits, hopping over children's feet and turning the stair corner to the balcony that wrapped around the room. When she got to the top, she turned left through an enormous pair of double doors leading away from the party. A few guests had wandered into this hall, but Clara hurried past them and through another set of doors into a cool, dark library.

She sighed in relief and leaned heavily against the wall. *Breathe in, breathe out,* she told herself. The fresh welling of sorrow from hearing her mother's favorite tune dulled. Her chest relaxed. There were no party guests here. She was alone.

An owl was perched on the back of a stately chair in one corner of the room. It hooted at her, yellow eyes glinting in the moonlight from a nearby window. Clara looked at it curiously before walking on through yet another pair of doors into what she considered the most glorious room of all in Drosselmeyer's manor: his workshop.

"Godfather?" Clara called.

The chatter of party guests echoed faintly from the great hall, muffled by the sound of inventions whirring and clicking in the workshop. Cogs rotated and pistons pumped. Trinkets and souvenirs from all over the world lay scattered in categorized piles. Clara had always felt safe here, surrounded by well-oiled machines and the whir of gears. Here everything made sense.

The owl hooted again and glided past. It landed on a workbench on the opposite end of the room, where a man in an impeccable suit, with dark skin and wild, grizzled hair, sat hunched. He looked up at the owl, and then to Clara as she approached. He smiled. One eye was covered with a patch, but his other eye was deep brown and kind.

"Hello, Clara," he said. "I was hoping you would turn up. I can't get this darned thing working."

He showed her what he was tinkering with: a complex golden model of a lake with two ceramic swans perched on top. Beneath the surface, supported by four golden pillars, was an intricate array of gears that were clearly meant to make the mechanical swans paddle their feet and flap their wings. But as Drosselmeyer flicked the model's switch, the swans flapped backward.

"You probably just need to reverse the mechanism," Clara suggested.

Drosselmeyer eyed her wryly. "That's what I'm trying to do, my dear. But despite there being two hundred people out there, not a single one of them brought a star-shaped screwdriver."

Clara rummaged through her pouch and produced the needed tool.

Drosselmeyer smiled. "I knew I could count on you. Here, you try. My hands are too large to fit inside anyway."

He handed Clara the machine. Without missing a beat, she began reworking the mechanism, shifting cogs and replacing gears. A moment later, she looked up.

"Here, try that."

Drosselmeyer flipped the switch, and this time, the swans' wings flapped in the correct direction.

"Brilliant girl!" He clapped. "You remind me of someone."

Clara couldn't help smiling. A teacher like Drosselmeyer had a way of making you want to make him proud.

"Now, young lady," Drosselmeyer continued, "why aren't you enjoying the celebration?"

"I need your help, Godfather. With this."

Clara produced the egg-shaped trinket box, and Drosselmeyer drew in a deep breath.

"Ah, I made that for your mother. When she first arrived here, I hadn't a clue what to do with a little orphan girl—old man like me—so I did the only thing I knew how to do. I made her this."

Drosselmeyer admired the egg as though pondering a distant memory. Clara supposed he must be thinking back to all those years ago, to the day her mother had come to the Drosselmeyer estate. She'd heard the story many times from her mother: how as a very young girl, when her parents had died in a tragic fire, Marie had arrived on Drosselmeyer's doorstep in the snow with nothing but a satchel, a doll, and the clothes on her back.

"And now it seems she's given it to you," Drosselmeyer mused. "Interesting, don't you think?"

"But without a key," Clara told him.

"Really?" Drosselmeyer peered into the lock. "Hmmm. A pin tumbler lock. Clever Drosselmeyer. You won't get into that with a star-shaped screwdriver."

"I know," Clara said. Her voice faltered a bit. "I tried."

Drosselmeyer read the look on Clara's face. His own expression softened. "You must miss her terribly," he said.

Clara didn't say anything. She just nodded.

"Sometimes it helps to talk about things, Clara." Drosselmeyer handed her back the precious egg. "Let the sadness out of your heart so it can mend."

Clara thought about this, gazing down at her mother's beautiful, mysterious, and final Christmas gift.

BONG!

The grandfather clock in the great hall suddenly chimed. It began playing an extraordinary melody, unlike any typical timepiece.

Drosselmeyer rose to his feet, the moment broken. "It's time for the presentation of presents," he said. "The guests won't be kept waiting. My dear, will you do me the honor?" He offered her his arm.

Clara took her godfather's arm and followed him out of the workshop.

As they stepped back into the merriment of the Christmas celebration, Clara couldn't help wondering what her own mother had thought upon seeing all of this for the first time, when she had been a young girl orphaned and all at once alone in the world. Had she felt joy? Sorrow? Curiosity?

And had she wondered, as Clara did now, if Christmas would ever again be as magical as it had once been?

CHAPTER 3
MARIE

Marie gazed at the looming manor before her. The hard snow crunched under her boots, and she shifted her weight while clutching a tattered knapsack and doll close to her chest.

Two constables spoke with the owner of the manor—a tall man with dark skin and an eye patch. Marie had seen him before in her parents' clock shop, but only from her hiding place under the counter where she used to play with her doll while her parents worked. She'd heard her parents say his name many times: Drosselmeyer.

That had been before the fire. Now the shop and her home were gone, and so were her parents. She'd spent the past week feeling very frightened, crying a lot at first, but now she was empty of tears. Scotland Yard's search for next of kin had come up woefully empty. Alas, Marie knew she had no other family. It had always been just her and her parents, working every day in the clock shop and retiring at night to the small one-room flat above. But for some reason, every time an officer suggested carting her off to the orphanage, whispers of the name "Drosselmeyer" popped up.

And now here she was, along with two constables, standing in the snow on the doorstep of the Drosselmeyer estate mere days before Christmas. What did it all mean?

"It's terrible, what happened," Drosselmeyer said to the constables. "But I don't understand. Her parents left her to me? As her guardian?"

"Well, not exactly," one of the constables replied. He was short and round, with a red, runny nose that he kept sniffing loudly in the cold. "Your name were all over their ledgers, though. 'Drosselmeyer' this and 'Drosselmeyer' that. One of the only things that survived the fire, 'cept for the girl."

"It was one of the only clues we had to go on," the other constable, a tall man with a mustache as dark as his black constable's cap, added. He suddenly looked to Marie, and she buried her face in her doll's hair.

"Tell him what you told us," the tall constable instructed.

Marie stared at him. Her breath made little clouds of steam above her doll's head.

"It's all right," the constable said a bit more gently. "Tell him what your parents told you, about the ledgers."

Marie swallowed. "They said they were important." She spoke very quietly. "When the shop caught fire, we all ran out. Father gave them to me. He said to keep the ledgers safe, for Mr. Drosselmeyer. Then they went back in to try and stop the fire." What she didn't add was that the roof collapsed before the firefighters arrived, and her parents never made it out from the blaze.

"She has no immediate family," the tall constable explained. "Her parents appear to have been private people, and nearly everything they owned was destroyed in the fire. But the child mentioned you knew them, and considering your—er—status, we thought it worth checking."

"If I would take her as my charge?" Drosselmeyer clarified.

"Ahem—yes." The constable coughed. "We would have contacted you sooner. But your valet informed us you were away on expedition until Christmas."

"It's terrible," Drosselmeyer murmured again in his gravelly voice. "Such a tragedy. I've been a customer of theirs for many years." The old man flipped through the ledger pages. "He'd say it was patrons like me who had an appreciation for the beauty of old mechanics that kept his shop running in an ever-changing world."

"So, you were close?" the tall constable prodded.

"Yes, in a manner of speaking," Drosselmeyer replied. "Her parents were more knowledgeable than most. And their clock shop was the only one in all of London that sold the tools I need for my inventions."

"Inventions, eh?" The ruddy constable chuckled. "What're you cookin' up in that there castle of yours? Some Frankenstein's monster?"

Drosselmeyer gave him a wry look before continuing. "I was very fond of Marie's parents. Her father and I even worked together on several projects. But a child . . . I've never considered . . . She truly has no one?"

Marie had been listening with interest to the conversation. Drosselmeyer turned to gaze at her with his unpatched eye, and she huddled her face down against her knapsack, clutching her doll even more tightly.

"What will happen to her?" he asked. "If no family is found?"

"Ain't *if* at this point," the ruddy-cheeked constable sniffed. "We've looked all we can. It's off to the orphanage now."

"You don't need to speak so loudly," Drosselmeyer admonished. "She does have ears."

"It makes little difference," the tall constable said, a touch more quietly. "Reginald is right. You were our last lead. Scotland Yard can't house her any longer. We'll drive her to the orphanage before dark." He looked to Marie and sighed. "Shame, though. I hate these sorts of rounds this time of year. Sad, very sad." He beckoned Marie. "Come, child. Back to the carriage."

Marie's shoulders slumped. She wasn't sure what the orphanage would be like, but she could tell from the looks on the men's faces that it probably wasn't good. She crunched back over the thick snow, her boots sliding on the icy mounds. As she passed Drosselmeyer, she slipped, landing hard on the ice. The cold stung bitterly against her stockings.

"Careful, child." Drosselmeyer helped her to her feet. "Bones are much harder to repair than gears." That was when he noticed the gleam of a pocket watch dangling from her knapsack. Engraved on the back was an ornate letter *D*.

He took hold of it, carefully opening the cover to reveal a tiny, motionless clock inside.

"I remember when I gave this to your father," he said. "As

thanks for his help repairing a particularly stubborn grandfather clock."

Drosselmeyer gazed pointedly into Marie's eyes. She stared back, without even meaning to. For some reason, she felt comfort as she did so. He was, after all, the last person left who had truly known her parents. Perhaps he was thinking the same thing.

The old man wound the pocket watch and gave it back to her. Then he took her tiny hand in his large, steady palm.

"Come along," Reginald huffed. "Into the carriage."

"There's no need for that," Drosselmeyer said. His hand never left Marie's.

"But we've told you," the tall constable insisted. "Scotland Yard can't house her any longer."

"Well, then." Drosselmeyer smiled kindly at Marie. "I suppose this will need to be her new home."

Several days later, it was Christmas morning. Young Marie sat at the breakfast table, wearing a simple yet pretty Christmas dress, eagerly eating a bowl of porridge. It was creamy and piping hot, the way her mother used to make it.

"Slow down there, or you'll get a tummy ache!" The cook tsked. "Didn't your parents ever feed you?"

"Yes," Marie replied quietly. "But they died."

The cook's expression changed suddenly. "Sorry, child," she said. "Didn't mean to bring that up, especially on Christmas morning. Here." She placed a basket of warm gingerbread biscuits on the table in front of Marie.

Marie's face lit up.

"I wasn't going to put these out until later," the cook said, "but what's the harm in an extra nibble or two? Just don't go eating the whole basket, or you'll turn into a right little sugar plum!"

"That's my doll's name." Marie held up her porcelain doll. She'd been clutching it with one hand in her lap beneath the table. In fact, Marie hadn't let go of her doll since arriving at the estate. The lovely toy had been a Christmas gift from her parents and had surely cost more than they could afford to spend on a plaything. It was one of her most treasured possessions.

"That's a very pretty name." The cook smiled. "Once you're finished eating, you can make your way to the library. Master Drosselmeyer is waiting for you."

Two bowls of porridge and several ginger biscuits later,

Marie walked with the butler up a staircase to the grand library at Drosselmeyer's estate. Even with the butler by her side, she couldn't help feeling very small and very alone up against the vast size of everything surrounding them. She had never seen such an elaborate home before—had never even imagined such a place could exist outside of a storybook. The wide stairs were covered with richly patterned runners, and massive chandeliers glowed above them with at least a hundred tiny gaslights each. Even the exotic wallpaper lining the halls seemed imposing. Up until now, Marie had spent most of her time at the estate huddled in her room, reading and rereading several fairy tales the servants had found for her in the library. All the staff had treated her very kindly, helping her find clothes small enough to fit her slight frame and preparing a soft, lovely bed. But as grateful as Marie was to not be in an orphanage, none of this felt real to her. The room, the estate, the servants, and even Drosselmeyer himself—it all felt oddly like an illusion that Marie feared might vanish at any moment. Even while safely tucked in her bed, warmed by hot water bottles so she wouldn't need to have a fire going in her room's hearth, she couldn't help feeling lost. The only things that seemed real to her were her doll and the stories she would read over and over again, the same way her mother used to read to her. At least they were familiar. Everything else about this new life was so . . . foreign. What place could a child like her—a simple watchmaker's daughter with no one and nothing left in the world—possibly have in all of this?

She hadn't seen much of Drosselmeyer since he'd told the constables she could stay. She knew from the servants that he traveled often on worldwide expeditions. But now that he was home for the holidays, they told her he spent most of his time in a place called "the workshop." Marie had heard her parents say he was an inventor. She wondered what sorts of things he invented.

Then, almost as if in magical answer to her unspoken question, an invention had mysteriously appeared outside her door earlier that morning—Christmas morning. She'd nearly missed hearing the faint knock. It was tentative, quiet as a whisper. Curious, she had crept to the door and cracked it open a tiny bit to peek outside.

The hallway had been empty, but resting on the floor was a shiny metal egg. Its casing was etched with intricate swirls and patterns, and the middle was sealed with a six-pointed star-shaped lock. It appeared to be a tinkered contraption of some kind. And attached by a red velvet ribbon was a tag, its message written in swirling calligraphy:

To Marie. Merry Christmas.

She marveled at it, wondering what it could mean.

Then the cook's familiar clunky footsteps had approached. The woman had come to see if Marie was feeling brave enough to venture down for breakfast in the dining room, the same way she had come to check every morning. And for the first time, curiosity overcame fear; Marie ventured out from her room.

Now Marie stepped through the large double doors to the library, holding the egg gently in her hands and her doll wedged in her arms. Drosselmeyer was there, seated in a tufted chair. A large bird—an owl?—perched on the seat's back. The butler bowed and left the room.

"Ah, young Marie!" Drosselmeyer closed the book he was reading. "Let me be the first to wish you a merry Christmas."

"Merry Christmas, sir," Marie said shyly. "But the cook already wished me merry Christmas."

"The second, then," he corrected.

"And the butler," Marie added.

Drosselmeyer chuckled. "Well, then hopefully it shall be merry indeed. I see you found your present?"

Marie held out the egg. "I did," she said. "Thank you, sir. But what is it?"

"All will be explained," Drosselmeyer said, a twinkle in his eye. "But first things first. Come, let me look at you. My goodness, I almost didn't recognize you. Mrs. Rosmund certainly has found you a fancy Christmas dress. Is this truly the same watchmaker's daughter I used to spot hiding underneath the shop counter?"

"I am, sir," Marie replied.

"The servants have been treating you well, then?" Drosselmeyer asked.

"Yes, sir," Marie answered. She clutched her doll, Sugar Plum, to her chest. "Thank you, sir."

"Come now," Drosselmeyer chuckled. "Do I look so old as to be called 'sir' so often?"

Marie shifted her weight and didn't reply.

Drosselmeyer laughed again. "Never mind, you needn't answer that. But seeing as you're living here now, there must be a more familiar name we can settle on. Wouldn't you agree?"

"Yes, si—" Marie started. "Um, I could call you 'Mr. Drosselmeyer'?"

Drosselmeyer shook his head. "No, no, that won't do. Let's see. I worked with your father as a business associate. So I suppose one could say we were brothers of the same trade. Perhaps 'uncle' is more fitting a title? How does that sound?"

Marie smiled at the thought of Drosselmeyer being connected to her father, like family. "I like that. Uncle Drosselmeyer."

"Fantastic." Drosselmeyer clasped his hands. "So then, young Marie, are you settling in nicely?"

"I am, si—Uncle," Marie corrected herself. "Your house is very large."

"Is it?" Drosselmeyer gazed about the library. "I spend so much time cooped up in here, I suppose I haven't wandered the halls myself in some time."

"I've been staying in my room, too," Marie added. "I—I don't want to get lost."

Drosselmeyer tilted his head, a touch sadly. "You will never get lost, child," he assured her. "Mrs. Rosmund mentioned she hadn't been able to pull you away from your storybooks. And I am sorry I have not been more available to you since you arrived. My work is rather time-consuming, and . . . I'm afraid that I am new to this. I've never been a father, you see. Traveled too much to have time for a family. I'm sure this must feel very different for you, too."

"Yes," Marie said quietly. "It does."

Sympathy filled Drosselmeyer's eyes. "You must feel very sad."

Tears prickled Marie's eyes. Since her parents had died, no one had really spoken of her feelings. There had been many hushed whispers around her, all ending with the words *poor child*. Everyone spoke about her, but not to her. Not until now.

"I miss them so much," she said softly.

Drosselmeyer allowed Marie to bury her face in his shoulder, staining his suit with tears. "I know this is hard." He patted her head. "But you will get through this. I promise you that."

"Do you really think so?" Marie sniffled.

"I do." Drosselmeyer nodded. "Come, there is something I need to show you."

He held out his hand, and Marie followed him through another set of double doors and into his workshop.

Upon entering, Marie gasped. The room was cavernous,

filled from floor to ceiling with whirring gears and gizmos. "Look, Sugar Plum!" she whispered to her doll. "It's as though we've stepped inside a machine!"

Drosselmeyer guided her over to the corner of the room, where an ornate golden grandfather clock stood. Marie gazed at the beautiful timepiece. Even as the daughter of a watchmaker, she had never seen anything quite like this. The top face of the clock looked almost like a globe, with large numbers printed against crackled glass. The bottom compartment was hollow, with gilt-edged windows giving full view of the interior mechanism. Wheels and gears nested together; heavy thunks marked the passing time. But where a pendulum ought to be, there instead was an exquisite figurine of a woman with an enormous skirt made entirely from gold. The skirt was sculpted with a split at the base, revealing even smaller figurines poking out. They rotated around a tiny track, each one clicking a step farther as the seconds ticked by. To Marie, they looked like tiny round-bellied dolls.

"Do you know what this is?" Drosselmeyer asked her.

"It's a clock," Marie responded.

Drosselmeyer nodded. "Yes, but not just any clock. The most intricate, tricky, confounding contraption I have ever encountered. This is the clock your father helped me mend."

"My father?" Marie asked.

"Yes," said Drosselmeyer. "When no one else in all of London could get it working properly, he had the golden touch. I have no idea of its origin—it was here at the estate when I arrived. But no matter how I tried, I couldn't get the gears working. Your father—he was determined. He worked for weeks on this clock until it was up and running just so."

Drosselmeyer knelt down in front of Marie, placing his hands upon her shoulders.

"I see your father in you," he said. "Both of your parents. Only a determined little girl could have made it this far. Will you stay strong for them? And for me?"

Marie sniffled and nodded.

"Good girl." Drosselmeyer gently wiped the tears from her cheeks. "Now, no more crying. It is Christmas morning. If there is one thing that is imperative on Christmas morning, it is joy. And presents."

Drosselmeyer reached over to his workbench and picked up a shiny key. He handed it to Marie and nodded to the egg's lock. "I'm afraid inventions are the only gifts I know how to make," he said. "But I hope you like it. Merry Christmas."

Marie carefully used the key to unlock the egg, and gently opened it.

"Oh!" she said. Inside was a tiny mechanism with miniature gears surrounding a bumpy cylinder. The gears began rotating, and the cylinder slowly spun. One by one, thin metal pins plucked along the cylinder's precisely arranged bumps, producing a tinkling melody.

"It's a music box!" Marie realized with delight. She couldn't help feeling a rush of excitement as the pretty song played. "You made this? For me?"

"I did," Drosselmeyer said. "Your father once told me that each winding gear or pumping piston has a story to tell about the person who made it. I'd like you to keep this music box, Marie, to remind you of your parents. They loved you very much. And when you listen to it, remember that their love is inside you, too."

Without thinking, Marie threw her arms around Drosselmeyer and hugged him. "Thank you," she said.

Drosselmeyer patted her head. "It is not much. But you are quite welcome."

Marie turned the music box in her hands in awe. It was

beautiful—perfect. Even more intricate than any of the watches or clocks she'd seen her parents work on.

"Could I make something like this, too?" she asked hopefully. "Could you teach me?"

"Now *that* is something I do know how to do," Drosselmeyer replied. "Would you like to learn how to tinker?"

Marie nodded. "I would like that very much."

"Then so you shall," Drosselmeyer said.

Marie beamed. She gazed around at all the whirling wheels and gizmos clicking about the room. To her, it almost seemed like magic.

Magic that she was going to learn how to do.

 CHAPTER 4
MARIE

The months passed quickly at Drosselmeyer's estate. The winter snow melted, giving way to cool spring rains and warm summer breezes. Marie settled into her new life. She quickly found that her uncle Drosselmeyer ran his estate like a well-oiled machine. Meals, lessons, and even free time were all meticulously scheduled by the servants. But Marie didn't mind. The servants were always kind, and Marie felt glad for the structure. She always knew what to expect.

The quiet moments at night when she was all alone with her thoughts were the hardest. She missed her parents terribly. Sleep came fitfully or not at all, filled with nightmares where she called out for them in the dark, only to hear her own cries echoing back. But she refrained from telling the servants, worried they might think her ungrateful.

"Marie, you have circles under your eyes again," they'd say.

"I'm all right," she'd always reply. "Thank you."

Sometimes, while playing in the garden, Marie would catch

the scent of roses and become overwhelmed by a memory of her father's carefully tended flowers growing in sunlit pots. Or she'd swear she could feel someone place a hand on her back while she played with her doll, the way her mother used to do when it was time for dinner. It was in those moments that Marie would run to find the precious music box Drosselmeyer had given her. She'd open it, listen to its pretty melody, and imagine that her parents' love was inside. "I love you, too," she'd whisper back.

What Marie enjoyed the most about living at Drosselmeyer's estate were her regular tinkering lessons. Those were entirely new, and her thoughts never drifted to sad places while she was working. Drosselmeyer had started her with the basics: watches, clocks, windup toys, and gadgets. But Marie was a fast learner, and each skill came easily. It wasn't long before Drosselmeyer had her helping him with his latest prototypes: motorized wagons; mechanized hot-air balloons; even a conveyor belt that wrapped around the length of the estate, allowing them to move items from room to room without taking a single step.

"Clever girl," Drosselmeyer would say to her at the end of each lesson, impressed. "If you don't slow down, I'll need you to start teaching me."

But Marie wouldn't slow down. Tinkering brought her purpose—and peace. With each new contraption, it was almost as though she had a tiny bit more control over the world. And, for a little girl whose dreams were filled with smoke and haze, that was a powerful feeling indeed.

Summer turned to winter. Christmas came and went. And then another, and another. Every year, Drosselmeyer would ask Marie what she would like for Christmas. "A party!" she'd always reply. So he would have the cooks prepare her favorite dishes, and ask the more musical servants to strike up a tune. Then he would whisk Marie to the great hall, dancing around the Christmas tree, pretending they were at a brilliant ball.

Marie grew taller, her hands steadier as she worked. Her governess moved her from primary school lessons to concentrated subjects. In the blink of an eye, three years had passed, and Marie was ten years old. She had grown to feel like she had been at Drosselmeyer's estate her whole life.

The one thing she missed, however, was other children. Few of Drosselmeyer's friends were young enough to have children around Marie's age. And while Marie was allowed to venture into town with the servants as often as her studies and tinkering would permit, making friends wasn't easy. Living at

Drosselmeyer's estate carried an air of mystery. People were intrigued by her—fascinated, really—but parents seemed wary of suggesting something so pedestrian as a playdate to a man as important as Drosselmeyer. And since children didn't stop by the mansion of their own accord, Marie found herself mostly alone.

But she didn't mind, not really. As long as she had her uncle and her inventions, she was content. And when she wasn't studying or playing with her doll in the garden, the servants knew where they could find her: Drosselmeyer's workshop.

One afternoon, after her lessons, Marie was tinkering with an especially complex invention. Drosselmeyer had been away on business for several days and wouldn't be home until the next morning. Marie used the opportunity to complete a new mechanism he'd been perfecting: a dancing ballerina that pirouetted across a gilded marionette stage. To the untrained eye, it would appear like a normal entertainer's puppet. But upon closer inspection, one would discover that this ballerina danced without strings.

Marie peered through her mechanic's loop, fine-tuning the last miniature screws.

"Almost done, Sugar Plum," she said to her doll, which was resting on the workbench beside her.

That was the one crutch she'd carried over from her old life: Marie never went anywhere without her doll. A year or two earlier she'd made the mistake of bringing her doll openly to school lessons. The governess had scolded her so sternly Marie didn't make that mistake again. Now she usually tucked her beloved companion away in her book sack, or even under her skirts if need be. Marie knew it was a bit childish. But Sugar Plum had been with her from the beginning, since even before the fire.

"There." Marie tightened the last screw and leaned back. The ballerina was complete. She removed the loop from over her eye and wound the tiny key on the doll's back.

The ballerina whirred gracefully to life, skimming across the marionette stage on two pink satin pointe shoes.

"It's perfect." Marie smiled proudly. "Uncle Drosselmeyer will be pleased."

Marie looked to where Sugar Plum sat slumped. The doll's porcelain limbs rested upon the workbench, its tuft of silky pink hair coiled atop its head. Beautiful, yet motionless.

"I wish I could make you dance, too," Marie said wistfully. "You'd look lovely." She glanced around at the various mechanical toys in the workshop. Bears and soldiers and one-monkey bands. They were fascinating, but certainly not as pretty as Sugar Plum.

Meanwhile, the dancing ballerina's key wound down. It tilted its head and lowered its arms, coming to a stop.

Marie studied the ballerina. Then she looked to Sugar Plum. Her doll had fabric joints at the elbows, knees, and wrists. *How simple it would be,* Marie thought, *to replace the fabric with gears.*

Marie looked to the ballerina. She looked to Sugar Plum.

"I wonder."

Early the next morning, Drosselmeyer entered his workshop. He was tired from his journey and intended to drop off his tools before retiring to his chambers. But to his surprise, the gas lamps in the workshop were lit, and Marie was fast asleep at the worktable, her head resting upon her arms.

"Marie?" he said, gently waking her. "Have you slept here all night?"

Marie stirred and cleared her throat. "I'm sorry, Uncle." Her voice was hoarse. "I didn't mean to fall asleep. I was working."

Drosselmeyer turned his attention to the worktable, where a lovely mechanized doll danced without strings. "I can see that," he replied. "You've gotten the ballerina to dance. Well done—"

The old man stopped. He gazed at the pink-haired doll dancing across the table.

"But this is not the ballerina we were working on." He sounded surprised. For Drosselmeyer, that was very unusual.

The doll pirouetted perfectly *en pointe*.

"Is this . . . your doll?" Drosselmeyer asked, amazed.

"Yes," Marie said proudly. "Isn't it grand?"

"But how on earth were you able to mechanize her?" Drosselmeyer watched as the doll did a perfect arabesque.

"It took me all night," Marie explained. She felt fully awake now. "But her joints were fabric, you see. I replaced them with gears. The inside of her porcelain was hollow, giving more than enough space for the mechanics. It was simple, really, once I started. Almost like she was meant to dance."

"Incredible," Drosselmeyer whispered.

"Do you really think so?" Marie asked, beaming with pride.

"I do indeed," Drosselmeyer said, his eyes fixed on the doll.

Sugar Plum turned to face him. Her head tilted.

"If I didn't know any better," he said, "I would almost think she had come to life."

The crowd clapped as a ballerina bowed and lightly stepped offstage.

"Stunning!" a party guest praised loudly. "Simply stunning!"

"Encore!" cheered a man in a tuxedo.

Drosselmeyer watched from the wings. Clara stood beside him. Every year there was always a grand performance of Christmas carolers to entertain the guests before the end of the evening. But this year, Drosselmeyer had opted for a Christmas ballet, complete with dancers dressed as fairies and nutcrackers.

"The dancers were beautiful, Godfather," Clara whispered.

Drosselmeyer smiled. "They were indeed. But the best part is yet to come."

The old man stepped onstage to many murmurs of anticipation.

"Ladies and gentlemen," he announced, "it is time for my

favorite part of Christmas, my favorite part of this evening. May I present . . . your presents!"

With a flourish, footmen threw open the grand glass doors leading into the manor's garden. Children whooped and raced out into the frosty air.

The garden grounds of Drosselmeyer's estate were truly a sight to behold: an intricate maze of flowers and greenery, some even blossoming in the wintertime chill. Towering Roman sculptures kept watch while children scampered this way and that, past the frozen garden ponds and around an ornate gazebo. In typical Drosselmeyer fashion, all was illuminated by rare Chinese lanterns gleaming red and gold. But the grandest sight of all was the colorful web of strings stretching out from the gazebo center and covering the entire garden.

"A cobweb party!" one of the children exclaimed, enchanted.

The strings crisscrossed this way and that, twisting around statues and weaving through bushes and branches. Attached to each string was a tag bearing a guest's name.

"My dear friends," Drosselmeyer announced, "children and children at heart. Find the string with your name, and it shall lead you to your present. A little work is required, as you can see. There's no doubt that life can be a puzzle. But I guarantee, there's always something interesting at the end. Good luck!"

An enormous cheer erupted from the crowd as old and young alike began to revel in the fun, searching for their names, slipping and sliding in the snow, and laughing in delight.

Drosselmeyer looked on, nodding in satisfaction. Then he noticed that Clara still stood by his side.

"There's a present for you, too, Clara," he encouraged her.

"Thank you," Clara replied, hesitating. "But can I go later?"

Drosselmeyer clasped her hands. "My dear Clara, it is Christmas Eve! A time of mystery and expectation. Who knows what could happen? I wouldn't wait if I were you."

At that, Clara grinned. If Drosselmeyer said it was important, then surely it must be.

She headed into the garden, her party heels crunching in the snow. Some guests had already discovered their presents and were playing with them in the center of the gazebo. Children munched on candy canes. Adults marveled at tiny windup trinkets as they sent them marching along the garden walls. One child even pulled along a wooden toy horse on wheels. Then Clara realized the child wasn't pulling it at all—the horse was motorized!

Clara traced her hand along the colorful web of strings. How would she find the one bearing her name? There were so many.

That was when she noticed one string different from all the rest—a golden thread, glimmering in the lantern light. It alone looked untouched by the crowd. She made her way toward it, hopping over a group of children playing jacks in the snow, until she reached the end of the golden string, wrapped around a statue of an angel. Her tag was there.

Clara, it read in swirling calligraphy.

She gave the thread a gentle tug, and it fell away from the statue easily, leading back toward the estate.

That's odd, she thought. Her string was the only one that led away from the garden. She followed it, carefully winding the loose end around her palm as she went. It led her back through the double doors into the great hall, up a staircase, and down a long corridor.

"My present must be hidden somewhere in the manor," she said to herself.

The hall was mostly empty now. A few children scampered about, chasing one another and playing with their presents. Clara followed her string intently. Suddenly, a nutcracker doll appeared out of nowhere.

"Look!" a young voice cried.

It was Fritz, waving his present. Drosselmeyer had gifted

him a handcrafted nutcracker soldier with a striking uniform and regal hat.

"A nutcracker soldier!" Clara exclaimed. "How handsome."

"I'm going to show Papa and Louise!" Fritz exclaimed before bounding down the stairs.

Clara laughed, happy to see Fritz having such a wonderful time. Then she looked back at her string. She wondered what trick her godfather had up his sleeve. Smiling, she reached out to grasp it and continued on her quest. She followed it around the balcony, down a hallway, and in through a long, empty corridor.

Clara looked back. She was all alone now, far from the party clamor. For a moment, she wondered if perhaps she had made a wrong turn. She had never been in this section of the estate. But no, her golden string stretched out in front of her, down the entire length of the hall.

Extremely curious now, Clara pressed on. This hallway was different from the others in the manor. Its floor was checkered with red, black, and gold hexagonal tiles, while peculiar wallpaper lined the walls. Clara looked more closely at the pattern. The wallpaper was decorated entirely with tiny mouse silhouettes against a red background.

At the end of the hall was a heavy, closed wooden door. The string ran underneath it.

"My gift must be inside," Clara said, perplexed. *What could be here?* she wondered. *A study? Perhaps another workshop?*

There was only one way to find out.

She turned the doorknob and pushed the door open. It creaked as though its hinges hadn't been oiled in some time. Beyond was another corridor, shrouded in darkness. The gold string continued into the shadows.

"What *is* Godfather's present for me?" Clara asked herself.

Had this been anywhere else, she would have started to feel nervous. But this was Drosselmeyer's manor. She trusted him, just as her mother had. He was quirky, yes, but ingenious and kind. Like a great inventor should be. Whatever surprise he had planned, it was sure to be extraordinary.

Clara ventured into the dark, farther and farther from the flickering glow of the gaslights in the hall. She held the golden thread securely with one hand, running her other hand along the wall of the corridor so she wouldn't lose her balance.

How strange, she thought, sniffing the air. The scent of pine needles wafted about her, far more fragrant and fresh than the garlands decorating the great hall.

A blast of cold air rushed past, strong enough to blow the loose wisps of hair about her face. "There must be an open window here somewhere." Clara peered as hard as she could into the darkness. But it was no use. There was no light in this corridor. The only thing keeping her steady was her hand brushing the wall.

Suddenly, she felt something strange. The wall that had been smooth a moment ago now felt rough, like unpolished wood. She took a few steps farther and reached out again. She felt something gnarled and twisted this time. Then Clara's hand passed over moss.

It was a tree trunk.

Where am I? Clara thought in surprise. *How can I be outside when the door in the hallway was on the second floor?*

Pine needles brushed her face. A branch snagged her hair. She pushed forward, holding tightly to the golden string, until, finally, she stepped out of the darkness of the corridor into the soft glow of moonlight.

Clara drew in her breath.

She was no longer in a corridor. Or in Drosselmeyer's estate.

She was in a snow-covered forest, surrounded by pine trees as far as the eye could see.

CHAPTER 6

MARIE

"Uncle, why do we not use this hall?"

Marie had been helping Drosselmeyer carry an array of old machine parts and half-finished inventions from a storage corridor in his estate. It was a strange-looking hall, with its red, gold, and black checkered floor. A peculiar pattern lined the wallpaper, but with all the cobwebs and dusty contraptions covering it, Marie couldn't quite tell what it was.

Drosselmeyer brushed off his hands, careful not to smudge his suit pants. Even while carrying odds and ends, he was still impeccably dressed.

"My dear," he said, "when you live to be my age, you will find that there are a great many things you have but do not necessarily need." He looked around at the walls and ceiling of the hallway, as though observing it for the first time. "I've lived in this manor for many years. But even I do not know all its secrets. Perhaps when I was a younger man I would have explored all the nooks and crannies. Now I prefer to spend my time in my workshop, where I'm at home."

"But this is part of your home," Marie pointed out.

"True," he said. "But it has served as a better home for my inventions while I'm not working on them."

Marie marveled at the long-untouched devices strewn about. Sewing machines with cogs and pistons attached to the pedals. A bicycle with a bellows appendage connected to a wood-burning stove. And were those steam-powered roller skates?

"Did you make all of these inventions?" she asked.

"Yes and no," Drosselmeyer admitted. "Some I created. Others I collected in my travels. But I tinkered with all of them, and you can be certain there is a story to each."

"How about that one?" Marie pointed to a miniature balloon hanging from a scrollwork hook. A tiny tin basket with a conveyor belt inside was attached to the balloon by strings.

"A mouse-powered hot-air balloon," Drosselmeyer explained. "So even our smallest friends can enjoy a bird's-eye view."

Marie giggled. "And that one?" She pointed to what looked like a pair of mechanized wings.

"Ah, the great aerial escape," Drosselmeyer said with a

twinkle in his eye. "A story from my younger years, but not a tale for today."

"And what about that, down there?" She pointed all the way down the hall. "The invention in gold. What is that?"

In the dim glow of the lamplight, Marie and Drosselmeyer could just make out the gleam of a golden contraption at the very far end of the hallway.

"Upon my word," Drosselmeyer said quietly. "What's that doing there?"

He began to pick his way over the dusty bits and bobs toward the end of the hall. When he reached the golden invention, he stopped.

"What is it, Uncle?" Marie asked, making her own awkward way over the mess. "It looks like—oh!"

Standing before them was the beautiful grandfather clock Drosselmeyer had shown Marie in his workshop when she'd arrived at the estate. But now, the entire clock was covered in a thick layer of dust, and the numbers appeared dim. It was as though the whole timepiece had gone dark, waiting to be lit from within with golden light.

"Isn't this . . . the clock my father helped you mend?" Marie asked.

"It is indeed." Drosselmeyer nodded slowly. "But I don't understand what it's doing here. I could have sworn it was still in my workshop."

"I thought so, too," Marie added. "I used to look at it every morning. But it's so dusty, it must have been here a long time. It's strange, Uncle. I don't remember missing it."

"And I don't recall moving it," Drosselmeyer said. "How very odd."

Marie had never heard Drosselmeyer speak in this manner. She glanced at his face. An odd expression crossed his features. Bewilderment?

"Then where does the door lead?" she asked.

Drosselmeyer looked down at her, confused. "Door?" he asked.

"Yes." Marie pointed. "The wooden door behind the clock."

Drosselmeyer returned his attention to the wall in front of them. His unpatched eye grew wide. A heavy wooden door stood behind the grandfather clock, imposing and sealed shut.

"Now that *is* something," he said. "I do not know where it leads, for I have never been inside."

"Should—should we open it?" Marie asked.

"Yes," Drosselmeyer answered. "I think we should."

Carefully, he and Marie slid the grandfather clock to the side. Its base groaned in protest, leaving thick streaks in the dust on the floor.

"Oh!" Marie exclaimed. Something moved from behind the clock!

Squeak! It was a large mouse. The rodent ran in a circle before scurrying away and disappearing under the piles of dusty inventions in the hall.

"Perhaps our furry friend already knows what is behind the door," Drosselmeyer said with a chuckle. "Let us find out as well." He took hold of the knob.

"On three?" he asked Marie.

They counted and together pushed open the heavy wooden door.

Dust plumed out. Beyond the doorway was shadowy darkness. No windows or light. Stepping through would be like stepping into the abyss.

"I don't like this, Uncle," Marie said, beginning to feel a bit unsettled. "Do you think it's dangerous?"

"Come, now," Drosselmeyer encouraged her. "The Marie I know is always up for an adventure. As long as I am with you, I promise you are safe."

He reassuringly placed a hand on her shoulder, and together they stepped through into the unknown.

At first, they couldn't see much of anything. But the farther they walked, the more their eyes adjusted to the dark. They found themselves in an impossibly long hallway. It went on and on, farther and farther from the checkered-floor corridor. A brisk breeze suddenly blew the wisps of hair back from Marie's face. *There must be a hole in the wall of the manor,* Marie thought.

"I see something," she said. "Up ahead."

A soft glow at the end of the tunnel became visible—pink at first, then orange and yellow.

"Uncle, the walls are made of tree bark." Marie reached out to touch the sides of the hallway.

Drosselmeyer did the same. "So they are," he said. "Very curious."

They continued along, the light growing brighter. The walls of the corridor seemed to fade, giving way to individual tree trunks. And with the rising sun, both Marie and Drosselmeyer realized where they were.

"Uncle, we're in a forest!" Marie exclaimed.

She was right. Stretching out before them a vast

landscape of evergreens. Grassy pathways matted with dew led between the trees. And the air was fresh with the scent of pine.

"The door has led us outside!" Marie said.

But Drosselmeyer shook his head. "There is no forest in London. We appear to have traveled . . . elsewhere."

"How is that possible?" Marie asked.

"I'm not sure," the old man replied. "Come, let's go a bit farther and see if some answers lie ahead."

Together, they pressed on through the trees. But no matter how far they went, they discovered only more questions. The forest appeared massive, filled with winding paths that wove between lush pine trees towering overhead, all stretching majestically toward the bright blue sky. Marie and Drosselmeyer took turns choosing which path to follow next, keeping careful track of the direction they went and leaving pine cone markers to avoid getting lost. It was a remarkable place, Marie thought. The trees shimmered impossibly green, vibrant and alive, with nary a brown pine needle or a fallen log in sight. She had never thought a forest could look so—perfect.

They continued wandering for nearly an hour without any further clarity on where they were. Then, finally, just as Marie's stomach began to rumble in anticipation of teatime, the trees thinned, and Marie heard the faint sound of rushing water up ahead.

"Do you hear that, Uncle?" she asked. "I think there's a river."

"Perhaps," said Drosselmeyer. "But to my ear, it sounds more like a waterfall."

They pushed past the last trees and entered the brilliant sunlight of the forest's edge, the thundering sound of water echoing louder and louder all the while, until they saw it: the end of the forest, and the beginning of everything.

"Uncle!" Marie exclaimed. "It's like a whole other world!"

Marie and Drosselmeyer had reached a grassy precipice overlooking a wondrous landscape, endless in reach and breathtaking in its purity. Fields of wildflowers stretched for miles, rippling with soft color. Distant mountains shimmered with the hint of snowcapped peaks. And wide before them, just a few yards away over the grass, was the edge of a massive chasm that dropped down hundreds of feet to a rushing river below. The canyon snaked around a central island, separated from the fields and mountains like its own perfect sanctuary, with a raging waterfall plummeting down into the abyss and connected to the mainland only by a single stone bridge spanning the expanse.

Not a person or animal stirred amid the magnificent sight. It was as though the entire landscape was uninhabited, save for one very prominent detail:

"A palace," Drosselmeyer breathed.

Rising high in splendor upon the island was a magnificent palace, sparkling with colorful stonework and swirling turrets. Windows dotted the towers, shimmering with crystal and glass. And the ornamental domes at the top of each spire looked, to Marie, almost like perfect dollops of ice cream atop cones. She felt her heart race at the impossible beauty of it all. It was like a vision from a storybook, a dream made real. Imagination brought to life.

"Where are we, Uncle?" was all she could say.

"I do not know," Drosselmeyer replied, equally astonished. "This is not what I expected when we entered the doorway. But now that we are here, it warrants further . . . exploration."

And that is just what Marie and Drosselmeyer did. Every day for nearly a month, in between tinkering and lessons, they would return to the door at the end of the hall and enter the magical world just beyond the estate walls. The landscape seemed to stretch on infinitely, with countless miles of fields and valleys and brooks to traverse. Even the central palace contained more rooms than could be explored in a single day. It was like an entirely new realm opened up through a doorway in a dusty, abandoned corridor, and that was what Marie and Drosselmeyer called this wondrous place: the Realm.

They had no idea *where* the Realm was, exactly. Having traveled the world, Drosselmeyer was quite certain this mysterious land didn't exist on any map. But they did discover three things.

First, the Realm was uninhabited, void of any animals or other people. Though someone had clearly built the palace, whoever that someone or something was had long since departed. The cavernous rooms sat vacant, without furniture or adornment. It was as though they lay quietly waiting for a new guest—or a new owner—to come fill them with life and memory.

Second, time moved much more slowly in the Realm than in the outside world. Hours spent wandering through the fields would take mere minutes back at the estate. Marie and Drosselmeyer could spend an entire day exploring and still be back in time for tea.

And third, things that existed in the Realm couldn't be

brought back to the real world. Marie had stumbled upon that discovery by accident. One day, while she and Drosselmeyer were enjoying a picnic lunch in the soft grass, she'd woven herself a crown of wildflowers.

"Ah, Marie, that is beautiful!" Drosselmeyer had said.

"Don't worry, Uncle," Marie had countered. "I'll make a crown for you as well!"

The old man had chuckled. "The best inventors never lose their spark of playful wonder. Always hold on to that."

Later, Marie and Drosselmeyer had headed back to the estate, both wearing their wildflower crowns. But the moment they stepped through the doorway and over the threshold into the real world, the delicately woven sprigs had vanished like dust dispersing in sunlight.

"Oh!" Marie had exclaimed. "Where did they go?"

Drosselmeyer patted his head. "I don't know." He looked back through the doorway. "I never considered trying to bring something back from the Realm into the real world. Curious."

"But weren't the flowers real?" Marie asked. "They were very real while I was working with them. Although . . ." She paused for a moment. "I do remember thinking I wanted blue flowers for your crown, but all I had to work with were pink ones. And then, suddenly, I spotted some blue flowers where I was sitting all along. It was strange, because I'd been certain there were only pink flowers there before."

"So, you imagined blue flowers, and they suddenly appeared?" Drosselmeyer asked.

Marie shrugged. "I'm not sure. Maybe?"

The old man nodded slowly. "Even more curious."

"But what does that mean?" Marie pressed, suddenly a bit worried that perhaps their fantastic discovery had been an illusion all along.

"I believe it means that things are possible inside the Realm which are not possible here," he answered.

"So it's not quite real?" Marie asked, disappointed. She had grown to love the Realm and the happy times spent exploring there with her uncle, and it didn't feel right for it to all be fake.

Drosselmeyer turned to look at her. "What makes you say that? On the contrary, it is extraordinary, and very much real in its way—made from pure imagination."

"Ah." At that Marie brightened. "So, do you think . . . perhaps I can make more things come to life in the Realm? Like the flowers!"

Drosselmeyer pondered her question for a long while. "I

suppose I don't see the harm," he said finally. "After all, imagi-nation is the birthplace of invention."

A wide grin spread across Marie's face. "Oh, thank you, Uncle! Thank you so much! Just think of how much fun it will be to make *new* things in the Realm. To see what's possible!"

The old man laughed to see Marie so jubilant. "I believe it is the beginning of a grand adventure," he said. Then he placed his hands on her shoulders. "Just always remember, only you can bring your dreams to life in the real world. And the real world only has one of you. Do not get so lost as to forget to come back."

"I won't, Uncle," Marie said. "I promise."

CHAPTER 7

CLARA

Clara couldn't believe her eyes. The golden thread had led her through the passageway and into an enchanting winter forest.

But where is this? she thought. *I've been all over London, and I've never seen a forest. And why is there so much more snow here than in the garden? Did it storm again while I was following the string? Could the snow have even fallen that fast?*

The questions raced through Clara's mind, seeming to echo without answer against the peaceful silence of the forest. The only thing that was certain was that her golden string continued through the thick trees, meaning that Drosselmeyer's gift was still waiting somewhere in the unknown.

"I suppose there is only one thing *to* do." Clara took a deep breath and trudged on. She pushed past prickly pine branches, her footsteps crunching in the snow until the golden thread led her to a clearing.

Clara gasped.

In the middle of the clearing was a most wondrous sight—a Christmas tree, grand and tall, shimmering with icicles and glowing red berries.

How beautiful! Clara scanned the boughs of the tree in astonishment. *It's . . . it's just like Mother used to do in the parlor, except real! Real berries, and real icicles!*

Clara felt incredibly touched. *How did Godfather do it?* she wondered. *It must have taken him ages to decorate this.*

Enchanted, Clara walked up to the tree and touched one of the berries.

"Oh!" she exclaimed.

The berry flitted away!

It wasn't a berry at all. It was a candy-colored firefly, glowing magically against the night sky. The tiny insect landed on Clara's nose, causing her to look at it cross-eyed. Then it buzzed back into the tree.

Delighted, Clara gave the tree a shake. A swarm of luminous fireflies wafted into the air, dispersing into the woods in a thousand twinkles.

"Incredible!" Clara clapped.

With the fireflies gone, the tree was empty now save for one shining gold ornament hanging high up on a branch. The ornament was connected to Clara's golden string, and it had a six-pointed star shape at the end.

The key to her mother's trinket box.

Clara felt her heart leap. "I should have known."

She reached up, standing on tiptoes to grasp the key. Her fingers were just about to touch it when—

Out of nowhere, a scruffy mouse slid down the branch and snatched the key up in its teeth! It scampered away.

"Hey, that's mine!" Clara yelped.

But the mouse was off, running deep into the woods.

"Come back here!" Clara yelled urgently. She picked up her skirts and sprinted after the rogue mouse as fast as she could. The little thief was getting away with the present—*her* present— the one thing that could unlock the secret of the egg and reveal her mother's final message. Clara's feet blistered in the uncomfortable party heels Louise had forced her to wear, but she paid them no mind. She had to get that key back!

Pine branches scraped across Clara's face and gnarled roots tripped her up as she ran. She could feel the welts forming on her cheeks, marring the lovely powder Louise had helped her apply. She was certain Louise would yet again scold her upon her return to the party. *For heaven's sake, Clara, just look at the state of you!* What *have you been doing?* Clara could almost hear her sister say. But she pushed the thought away. Keeping the mouse in sight was the only thing that mattered. Luckily, its brown fur stood out against the white snow. And Clara followed it like a beacon, not even slowing to catch her breath.

The mouse ran all the way to the edge of the forest, and as it burst from the trees, Clara thought for sure she could chase it down in the clear fields. But when she reached the end of the tree line, she gasped and instinctively skidded to a stop.

Stretched out before her was a foggy landscape. In the shadows, she could just make out the dim shapes of torn-down buildings. Crumbling walls and broken machinery. The ruins of a city, fallen to dereliction, moss, and weeds.

Clara didn't like this. It didn't feel right. An abandoned corner of London certainly wasn't somewhere her godfather would lead her to. She must have gone off course. After all, the mouse had led her very far astray. But Clara had to get that key back. It was the only way to uncover the final message her mother had left her.

At the edge of the ruins stood an ugly, gnarled tree. Its bark hung ragged and decaying along the trunk. Any leaves or foliage were long gone. The mouse sat on one of the barren branches, peering at Clara. One of its beady eyes was sealed shut with a scar. The golden key dangled from its teeth.

"That key belongs to me," Clara declared. She moved toward the furry thief. But then, ever so slightly, the entire tree wavered. It shifted. Clara froze as a thousand eyes opened and stared at her. The tree was *covered* in mice.

Clara recoiled in disgust. Mechanized mousetraps might have been one of her specialties, but she had never seen so many rodents in one place.

Even still, she refused to leave. Nothing could make her retreat without that key.

One of the mice advanced toward her, teeth nipping. Then another, and another. Clara held her ground . . . but a mouse jumped and landed on her shoulder! Clara yelped, smacking it off.

"Shoo! Go away!"

More mice leaped. Their claws snagged her dress. Several mice tangled in her hair!

"Get off! *Get off!*" Clara screamed. She swatted and grabbed at the mice as they swarmed her, but they kept advancing, forcing her away from the forest and toward the ruins of the city.

"Please!" Clara cried. "I just want my key!"

Suddenly, the thundering sound of horse hooves echoed in the darkness. A young man dressed in a military uniform galloped out from the fog, sword brandished, head held high.

"Have at you!" he challenged the mice.

The valiant soldier swiped, slicing through the writhing mass of mice attacking Clara. The mice screeched in fury, scattering at the sting of the soldier's weapon. Several moved to come at him again, but the soldier swung once more, sending all the mice reeling back into the night.

Clara ran a hand through her hair, making sure there were no lingering rodents there. She turned to the soldier gratefully.

"Captain Phillip Hoffman." The soldier secured his sword and bowed to Clara. "Don't know what you're doing here, but hop up. We need to go."

He extended a hand to help Clara climb on his steed. She hesitated.

"Go?" she asked. "I can't. That mouse has my key!"

"Big admirer of bravery under normal circumstances," Phillip replied. "But believe me, this is not the place to linger in a party dress."

"You can talk," Clara huffed, eyeing his unusual uniform. She knew her godfather had many acquaintances from all over the world, but this soldier's outfit wasn't like any military uniform she had ever seen. It almost looked like the costume Fritz's nutcracker doll had been wearing! "I didn't see the words 'costume party' on the invitation," she said.

Phillip frowned. "What invitation?"

"To the Christmas party, of course," Clara told him. "And I'm not leaving without my key!"

Just then, Clara and Phillip heard the unmistakable high-pitched squeaks of a thousand mice. They turned. In the fog, the rodents were regrouping, climbing on top of one another and lashing their tails together in a giant writhing mass.

"What are they *doing*?" Clara asked in revulsion.

The mice continued to swarm, clambering on one another's backs, their claws digging into each other's fur. The mouse with the scar that had stolen Clara's key climbed up into the very center. The entire mass heaved, forming the shape of one enormous mouse with vicious swiping claws and gnashing teeth.

"They're forming the Mouse King," Phillip warned. "We need to get out of here. Now!"

But it was too late. The Mouse King took a hulking step forward, flicking its slithering tail made up of a thousand beady-eyed rodents. Phillip's horse reared and bolted in terror. The brave soldier drew his sword, but it was too late. The Mouse King struck him, sending him sprawling back upon the snowbank, dazed and weaponless.

The Mouse King howled. It loomed over him, ready to strike.

Clara watched, frozen. What could she do? She had to save him!

She looked around frantically for something—anything!—to use as a weapon. But the only things even remotely sharp were Phillip's sword, out of reach, and her blasted pointy party shoes.

Her shoe! Without really thinking, Clara grabbed a shoe from her foot and hurled it at the center of the writhing Mouse King.

Bull's-eye! The pointed heel struck the scar-eyed mouse, sending it flying. It shrieked in anger as it disappeared into the fog. Clara's key flew from the mouse's mouth and vanished among the city ruins.

The enormous Mouse King wavered. Without their central leader controlling it, the mice were off-balance. They scrambled to re-form, but the distraction had allowed enough time for Phillip to regain his composure. He gripped his sword and sliced fiercely at the creature until more and more mice were knocked from the group. Disorganized, they retreated into the forest.

The last mouse squeaks faded into the trees, and just like that, Clara and Phillip were left alone in the silence.

Clara retrieved her shoe. She looked at it with new eyes.

"They do have a use after all," she murmured.

Phillip dusted off his uniform, taking a moment to compose himself. Then he flashed Clara a wry half grin. "My first rescue of a damsel in distress, as it happens."

"Me, a damsel?" Clara asked incredulously. "Didn't *I* rescue *you*?"

"Well, I suppose it was about fifty-fifty. You're pretty good with a shoe."

Now Clara smiled. She liked that Phillip was direct. He wasn't at all like the rowdy boys she was used to seeing in town, with their marbles and jacks and tricks. And he was certainly the youngest soldier she'd ever encountered.

"I'm Clara," she introduced herself. "And I think my key went somewhere over here."

She began to trek deeper into the crumbling city. Phillip chased after her.

"No, wait!" he exclaimed. "This is not a place to stay and look for keys. They'll be back, and not just them."

"It's important," Clara insisted, scanning the shadows.

"Important enough to risk your life?" Phillip asked.

Clara gave him an odd look. "What sort of soldier lets a few mice stop him?"

"A *few* mice?" Phillip asked in shock. "You're either very brave, or you've got no idea what—"

He stopped, as though a terrible thought had occurred to him.

"Oh, no. You're not from the Realms, are you?"

Clara frowned. "The Realms?"

In one swift motion, Phillip grabbed Clara and pulled her behind a large, crumbling stone. He clamped a hand across her mouth. Clara gave a muffled cry in protest, but he held her fast.

"Be very, *very* still," Phillip urged quietly.

Clara was about to struggle when, in the distance, they heard it. Faint at first, then growing louder. Manic, babbling laughter, as though a dozen horrid jesters were hurtling toward them through the sky. Before Clara could figure out what was happening, an entire swath of dead tree branches looming over the city's remains peeled back, as though pulled aside by a massive creature. *Something* was looking for them.

"What—?" Clara choked out in horror.

"When I say 'now,'" Phillip whispered, "run for the forest."

The thing that had pulled back the trees advanced toward them. It was only then that Clara realized what it was—a hand! An impossibly large white porcelain hand. It swooped down through the fog, missing them by inches!

"Now!" Phillip cried.

He and Clara bolted from their hiding spot, sprinting for the tree line. The lunatic laughter followed them. Phillip raised his fingers to his mouth to let out a shrill whistle, and in a flash, his horse came galloping out from the shadows. Phillip swept Clara up onto its back, and they thundered through the trees. Leaves swirled. Branches crashed. And all the while, the maniacal laughter echoed at their backs.

What is happening? Clara thought desperately as they rode, the cold wind biting at her skin and causing her eyes to tear. *Am I dreaming? How is any of this possible?*

Phillip and Clara rode for a long, long time. Finally, his horse out of both breath and energy, Phillip slowed the steed to a walk.

"I think we've outrun them," he panted.

"What was that?" Clara asked in disbelief.

"*That* was Mother Ginger," Phillip replied. "A monster who rules the Fourth Realm. Which is why no one ever goes there. You're jolly lucky I noticed you were in trouble from my outpost when I did. What were you thinking, being there on your own?"

"But I was at my godfather's house," Clara insisted. "In London."

"Well, you're not in London now," Phillip said.

"Not in—wait, stop." Clara hopped off the horse, extremely frustrated. None of this was making any sense. "First those mice, and then Mother Ginger, and now I'm *not in London*?"

Phillip stared at her, seeming to be a bit lost for words. "Yes," he replied simply.

Clara shook her head. "I'm beginning to think my sister is right and I really am the mad one in the Stahlbaum family."

"*Stahlbaum?*" Phillip gasped. He suddenly hopped down from the horse and bowed low. "Your Majesty. I did not realize you were Marie's daughter."

Clara's heart leaped at the mention of her mother. "You knew her?" she asked, stunned.

"Of course," Phillip said. "This is her land. She created the Four Realms. And if you are her daughter, then we must make haste. You are not safe here. We must hurry to the palace."

"But Phillip, please," Clara pleaded. "I don't understand. What *is* all this?"

"Come!" Phillip helped her back astride his horse and spurred it on. "I will show you!"

CHAPTER 8
CLARA

Clara could scarcely believe her eyes as she and Phillip crashed out of the forest and into the brilliant daytime sunlight. It had been night just a short while ago at her godfather's house. But here, the sun rose high in the sky, shining as though it were midday. The mist and shadows of the decrepit Fourth Realm receded behind them, and Phillip brought his stallion to a halt at the edge of a precipice overlooking the grand majesty that was . . .

"The Realms," Phillip said proudly.

"Oh," Clara breathed. Stretched out before them was a land unlike any she'd ever imagined—a vast kaleidoscope of vibrant beauty and life.

"There's the Land of Flowers," Phillip said.

He pointed to a valley bursting with color. Endless rows of roses, lilies, and daffodils grew in carefully orchestrated gardens. Cottages and windmills dotted the landscape, covered in lavender and ivy. Cheerful songbirds flitted about, skimming the tops of the flower fields and causing the blooms to open in all their glory before gently folding back up into delicate buds.

"And the Land of Snowflakes." Phillip pointed over the valley's mountaintops to the second realm.

Beyond the peaks lay a twinkling winter village of ice and snow, centered atop a frozen glacier. Church spires and rooftops glistened with frost, and the icy landscape was so smooth it almost seemed to reflect the brilliant blue sky like a perfect mirror.

"And finally, the Land of Sweets," Phillip said.

Clara followed his gaze. The third realm was an entire city made up completely of delightful candy confections. Gingerbread houses. Candy cane bridges. Peppermint cobblestone. Even the roof tiles were iced with frosting, and the chimney stacks puffed plumes of marshmallow fluff.

"They're incredible," Clara said, mesmerized. She could hardly find the words to describe what she was feeling. This world—these realms—were a vision straight from a fairy tale. And in that instant, she had the strangest feeling of déjà vu. A distant memory tugged at the back of her mind, floating and elusive, a wisp she couldn't quite grasp. Flowers and snowflakes and sweets—the pattern sounded familiar, but she just couldn't remember where she'd heard it. Perhaps in a story, long ago? Maybe that was where her mother had drawn her inspiration from?

My mother, Clara thought over and over again. *My mother created all this, in secret, without us knowing.* For one of the first times in her life, Clara was speechless.

"There is the palace," Phillip spoke beside her. He pointed to a magnificent castle in the center of the Realms. It overlooked all, towering like a regal guardian. Four long bridges connected the castle courtyard to each of the realms, though the bridge leading to the desolate Fourth Realm was interrupted by a massive raised drawbridge. Beneath the palace thundered a great waterfall, which powered mighty water turbines that poured deep into a misty chasm.

"That is where we must go," he said. "The regents will be very eager to meet you, Clara Stahlbaum."

"The regents?" she asked.

Phillip smiled. "Your mother's closest companions."

Clara drew in her breath. Closest companions?

How could there have been so much to her mother that she had never known?

Phillip spurred on his horse, and together, they rode across the bridge from the dark forest and into the light-filled beauty of the Realms.

Guards lowered the massive drawbridge, admitting them into the palace courtyard.

"The drawbridge is the only thing keeping us safe," Phillip explained. "As long as it is raised, Mother Ginger and her mice cannot leave the Fourth Realm."

Villagers' heads turned as Clara and Phillip trotted past, curious to see this new visitor. Clara marveled at their attire. Spun-sugar dresses. Rainbow-colored bows and stockings. To Clara, they seemed like beautiful dolls from a toy store come to life.

Phillip tethered his horse in the courtyard and they entered the palace. Clara had never seen anything like it. Intricate adornment represented each of the three remaining realms. Topiaries of flowers spiraled around perfectly chiseled ice sculptures. A grand chandelier made entirely of spun sugar hung overhead. And sunlight filtered through crystallized candy windows, casting rainbow reflections upon the frosty mirrored floor.

Phillip led Clara up a wide staircase, and a trumpet blare

announced their arrival. Guards opened two enormous double doors, admitting them to the palace throne room.

Inside, four thrones were purposefully placed before four windows, each looking out over one of the realms. Three of the thrones were occupied; the fourth remained conspicuously empty. And at the center of the room stood a glass case with a delicate crown resting inside on a velvet pillow.

"Your Excellencies," Phillip said to the regents. "May I present Miss Clara Stahlbaum?"

Though Clara was normally calm in the face of scrutiny, her heart gave a little leap as the regents turned toward her. She was about to meet for the first time the people her mother regarded as her closest friends—all while having never known they existed until a few moments before.

Clara's eyes grew wide as the regents turned. She had never seen royalty quite like them. On one throne sat the Snowflake Regent, wrapped in thick furs. His hair draped in snow-white coils about his chiseled features, and icicles hung low across his brow like frosty bangs.

The opposite throne was occupied by a much less imposing man—the Flower Regent. He wore a suit made entirely of petals, and an elaborate floral arrangement crowned his head. His green eyes flashed with a mixture of excitement and intrigue.

"Is it true? Is it true?" the Flower Regent suddenly exclaimed, hopping down from his throne. "How marvelous, how—"

"Hawthorn, please," the Snowflake Regent interrupted him. "Calm yourself."

"Sorry, sorry," Hawthorn apologized. "Hawthorn, Regent of the Land of Flowers, at your most humble service."

Hawthorn grasped Clara's hand and kissed it.

"Oh," Clara said, startled.

The Snowflake Regent stepped forward. "Shiver, Regent of the Land of Snowflakes," he introduced himself with an elegant bow. "Ma'am, an honor."

"I—thank you," Clara replied.

"And the Regent of the Land of Sweets," Shiver continued, gesturing to the third regent still seated upon her throne. "Sugar Plum."

Clara watched as Sugar Plum rose gracefully. She felt herself somehow to have already met this beautiful woman, though she was certain she never had. The Sweets Regent was a vision of perfection—beauty beyond compare. Her porcelain skin looked strikingly smooth against her dazzling pink gown. Crystallized sugar sparkled about her bodice and shoulders. Her lips were berry red, her eyes chocolate brown. And her pink hair coiled in a delicate pouf above her head like cotton candy.

"How lovely to meet you," Clara said.

Sugar Plum swept forward, lightly, like a ballerina. She placed both her hands upon Clara's shoulders and studied her, looking deep into her eyes.

"I never thought this day would come," Sugar Plum said quietly.

Clara opened her mouth to reply, then closed it. She wasn't sure what to say.

"Tell us, we long for news," Sugar Plum continued. "How is our queen—dear Marie?"

"My mother?" Clara asked, taken aback.

Sugar Plum nodded. "We miss her so."

"I—" Clara stammered. "You don't know?"

The regents looked at her expectantly. Clearly, they did not.

"My mother is—she died," Clara said.

The regents gasped.

"Marie, dead?" Hawthorn spluttered.

Shiver shook his head, icicle bangs tinkling. "We are so sorry for your loss."

"Our loss," Hawthorn interjected. Tears formed like dew-drops at the corners of his eyes.

"The loss, dear man, is everyone's. But particularly this young lady's," Shiver chastised him.

"Yes, yes, of course." Hawthorn struggled to regain his composure.

Meanwhile, Sugar Plum's face was frozen in disbelief. Her eyes grew distant, reflecting perhaps on a long-ago memory.

"To leave life so young," she whispered. "Oh, Clara, she was the most beautiful, wonderful—she meant everything to us. And we never even got to say goodbye."

A delicate tear rolled down Sugar Plum's cheek.

"I'm so sorry," Clara said. She had become so accustomed to the whispers of condolences surrounding her family, she'd never thought what to say to someone else struck by the same grief as she for the first time.

Sugar Plum's eyes focused. "Sweet girl." She touched Clara's cheek. "Comforting us when we should be comforting you."

"So, you've come to guide us, Clara?" Hawthorn asked expectantly. "Take over your mother's crown?"

"I—no," Clara started. "I'm afraid I didn't know about any of this. It's more of an accident that I'm here, really. My mother left me a Christmas present. A trinket box."

Clara withdrew the egg from her tool pouch. At the sight of it, Sugar Plum's eyes grew wide.

"May I?" she asked.

Sugar Plum grasped it delicately yet eagerly before Clara had a chance to respond. She turned it over in her hands. "Exquisite," she breathed. "So typical of your dear mother."

"And then, somehow, I found myself in the Fourth Realm," Clara continued. "A nasty mouse with a scar took the key that opens the box, and—"

"A key!" Hawthorn suddenly exclaimed. "Did you hear that, Shiver? A key! A *key*! Is it the same key, Sugar Plum?"

Sugar Plum studied the egg. She ran a delicate finger over the six-pointed star lock.

"Could it be *the* key?" Shiver asked with anticipation.

CHAPTER 9

MARIE

Summer turned to fall at Drosselmeyer's estate while Marie continued her daily adventures. Seasons didn't seem to exist in the Realm. It was always the same perfect temperature and same perfect weather, making it easy to lose track of time.

After her flower discovery, Marie had been very eager to see what other extraordinary things she could make. But try as she might, she found she couldn't create things just on a whim. The magic seemed to appear and vanish of its own accord, and when she least expected it. If she were in a particularly adventurous mood while heading off to explore, entire fields of blossoms would suddenly open in a brilliant kaleidoscope of color, welcoming her at the start of her journey. Other times, if a sad thought or memory occurred to Marie while she was there—like when she thought of her parents, or felt frustrated by a tinkering project gone wrong—the sky clouded over ever so slightly and a drop of rain would fall.

But if she tried to force something to happen, or to will it to exist—well, it just didn't work that way.

Back at home, business ventures began to draw Drosselemeyer's attention away from visiting the Realm with Marie as often. Inventions needed his focus, and he found that his thoughts were always pulled back to his work. So Marie started to visit the Realm alone, taking her Sugar Plum doll with her whenever she went.

Little by little, she brought her own tinkering contraptions over from her uncle's workshop to perfect in the Realm. Since time moved so much more slowly there, she found she was able to tinker for ages in the golden sunlight streaming through the palace windows without having to worry if she was spending too much time away from her studies. It was a grand plan until, one day, she returned home from a twenty-four-hour building extravaganza in the Realm, only to discover it was still mid-morning and she had a whole day's worth of school lessons ahead of her. After many yawns and an ill-timed snooze that earned her a stern lecture from her governess, Marie determined that she would need a proper bedroom in the Realm if she were going to continue spending so much time working there.

"Are you certain Master Drosselmeyer requested this furniture to be moved to the end of *this* hallway?" the servants had asked Marie, very confused, when they helped her haul a spare guest bed down to the end of the checkered hall aboard a dolly.

"Yes." Marie had nodded seriously. "It's very important. Crucial to the success of his inventions."

The servants looked at one another, even more confounded. But none of them seemed to want to question Drosselmeyer's orders.

Marie eyed the bed, with just a simple spread and one pillow resting on top. "And he said we'll need more pillows," she declared.

Soon Marie had fashioned a cozy little bedroom all her own in the Realm palace. It had taken a decent amount of effort to get it set up, from attaching a tinkered engine to the dolly so she could single-handedly transport the furniture through the forest, to then inventing a pulley elevator to haul it up to the top of the palace tower. But it had all been worth it. Everything looked just right. There was a pretty canopy, and a soft bedspread. All the pillows she'd "borrowed" from throughout the manor gave it a regal appearance. She'd even lined her palace bedroom windows with pink drapes and painted flowers along the walls like watercolor wallpaper.

"It's perfect," she said to Sugar Plum happily, admiring her handiwork. "Now I can spend as much time as I like here. Days, weeks. Maybe even more." She gazed around her peaceful room and out through the window overlooking the vast Realm landscape.

"It's too bad Uncle isn't here to see this," she said, a touch wistfully. "I wonder what he's up to in the real world right now."

Just then, something caught Marie's attention from the corner of her eye. Something that made her turn her head slowly and caused an odd feeling to creep through her chest.

"Sugar Plum . . . what is that?" she asked.

Visible on her bedroom wall, right where she had painted a bouquet of flowers, was the faint outline of a doorway. It was nearly hidden, but with the golden beams of afternoon sunlight streaming through the tower window just so, the outline was unmistakable.

"Another doorway," Marie breathed. "How did I not see it before?"

She wondered what this new bit of mystery from the Realm could mean. Had the door suddenly appeared? Had it been there all along? Had the Realm only now wanted her to see it?

And, most importantly, where did it lead?

The sunlight shifted, reflecting off Sugar Plum's glass eyes.

Marie took a deep breath. "There's only one way to find out."

"You won't believe it, Uncle! You won't believe it!"

Marie dragged Drosselmeyer along through the Realm, straight toward the palace.

"Slow down, child." Drosselmeyer loosened his collar. "I'm not as young as I look, you know."

"But you don't understand—this is incredible!" Marie pulled him along through the palace's grand hall and up the stairs to one of the very top towers, where she had furnished her cozy bedroom.

"Is this your bedroom?" Drosselmeyer asked in surprise when he saw the setup. "How lovely. I had no idea you'd been furnishing the rooms for yoursel—are those my pillows?"

"Never mind the pillows, Uncle," Marie insisted. "This—this is what I wanted to show you!"

Marie threw open the door that had mysteriously appeared in her bedroom wall and led Drosselmeyer up a short flight of stairs to a cavernous room filled with whirring gears, cogs, and pistons. Marie watched her mentor marvel at the mechanisms surrounding them, almost the same way she had marveled at his workshop the first time she'd seen it.

"Incredible," Drosselmeyer breathed. "You've created an invention room inside the palace."

"No, Uncle, it's better!" Marie exclaimed. She guided him over to a wall where several windows were covered with heavy closed drapes. "Look!"

She threw open the curtains.

Drosselmeyer gazed out the window. Through the crackled glass, he was just able to make out the view to the outside. There was an image printed on the window, warped and blurry. He studied it closer—it was an impression of a number, written backward, upon the glass. Then he saw the view beyond and realized they were not looking through a window to the outside landscape at all.

"Is that . . . my workshop?" he asked in disbelief.

Marie nodded enthusiastically. "I couldn't believe it when I first saw it, either!"

"But where—" Drosselmeyer looked around them at all the moving gears and mechanisms. Then he heard a familiar chime.

"Are we inside the grandfather clock?" he asked.

"Yes!" Marie cried. "Do you remember how we moved the grandfather clock back to your workshop? Somehow, the Realm has made it possible to *see* back into the real world through it! Like a window!"

"Or a portal," Drosselmeyer whispered. "Remarkable. You made this? Constructed the grandfather clock mechanism inside this room to act as a portal?"

"No." Marie shook her head. "I—I think the door might have been here all along and I just didn't notice it."

"Then that would make two of us," Drosselmeyer said. "For I certainly never noticed it as well."

"I did wonder what was happening in the real world when I first saw the doorway," Marie realized. "Maybe . . . maybe that's what helped me to see it. Is that even possible?"

Drosselmeyer pondered her question for a while. "Perhaps," he said slowly, "you have developed a deeper connection with the Realm. One that is unique." He returned his attention to the whirring gears around them. "And I daresay there are many more mysteries of this special place yet to uncover."

The appearance of the grandfather clock portal renewed Marie's eager spark to return to the Realm more and more often in hopes of discovering even more hidden bits of magic. But just as before, the Realm had a way of keeping its secrets to itself. No more unexpected revelations popped up, despite Marie's keeping a keen eye peeled for any hint, or thinking very focused thoughts and then whirling around to see if her imagination had brought them to life.

In time, she returned to her usual pattern. She would start her day with breakfast at the estate, and then hurry to Drosselmeyer's workshop to collect her latest contraption to tinker with in the Realm. Only now she had the advantage of peeping back into the real world every so often to keep track of how much time she had been away.

The palace rooms grew cluttered with her tools and trinkets, bits and bobs of different machines and gizmos. Her skills grew advanced—even more advanced than Drosselmeyer's, the old man would note. She had fashioned a cloak conveyor belt to run along the palace walls, just like the one at the estate. (Should any guests ever arrive for a grand ball, she liked to fancy.) She filled the palace kitchen with steam-powered iceboxes and self-replenishing wood-fired ovens. After a particular burst of inspiration, she even invented a motorized bicycle, perfect for traveling back and forth quickly from the palace, across the bridge, and to the real-world doorway so she wouldn't need to walk.

Whenever she completed a new invention, Marie would peek out through the grandfather clock window to see if Drosselmeyer was in his workshop so that she could run and bring her mentor to see her latest creation. But with time passing so slowly in the Realm as compared to the real world, Marie noticed that, more often than not, her uncle had stepped away to complete other business.

On one such occasion, Marie sat in her palace bedroom alone with her Sugar Plum doll.

"It sure is quiet here, isn't it, Sugar Plum?" Marie asked, a bit sadly. She wound up the key on Sugar Plum's back. The doll began dancing gracefully across the bed.

Marie glanced around her bedroom, decorated with flowers and trinkets and shelves filled with toy friends so she wouldn't feel lonely.

Except . . . she *was* lonely. It was always just her in the

Realm. She still didn't have any real friends back at home. Her governess had commented more than once that she would benefit from playing with children her own age. But between her studies and tinkering lessons and all the time she spent creating things in the Realm, there wasn't much chance for meeting new children. And Drosselmeyer was the only other person who knew about the Realm. They had both agreed long ago that it was a secret best kept between them. They had no idea what would happen if too many other people knew about a secret world hidden within the manor walls. Would they come for it? Try to take it away? Destroy it? Perhaps a bit selfishly, neither she nor Drosselmeyer wanted outsiders tinkering with what was their greatest tinkering possibility of all—pure imagination.

Still, Marie sometimes wished she had *someone* other than her uncle to share it with. Someone her age, who could play with her in the world she had created. Someone who would love it the same way she did.

"At least I have you," Marie said to her doll. Sugar Plum's key wound down, and the doll came to a stop with its head tilted inquisitively to the side, as it always did.

"You've been with me since the beginning," Marie continued quietly. "Wouldn't it be lovely if you were real, too?"

Sugar Plum seemed to stare at Marie, eyes unblinking.

"If you were real . . ." Marie repeated thoughtfully to herself. She thought back to her uncle's words when they had first discovered the Realm. *Things are possible inside the Realm that aren't possible in the real world.*

Marie glanced over to the door leading to the grandfather clock portal.

Perhaps you have developed a deeper connection with the Realm. And I daresay there are many more mysteries of this special place yet to uncover.

Marie took hold of her doll. She looked at the gears, the windup key. She was suddenly reminded of the music box Drosselmeyer had made her so many years ago, when she was a lonely orphan come to live at the estate. A perfect tiny machine, filled with love, and memory, and all operated by a key.

"I have an idea, Sugar Plum," Marie said slowly. "But for this to work, I'm going to need a lot more parts."

The next several months passed in a blur. Marie spent entire weeks in the Realm working on her invention. Even

Drosselmeyer started to notice her absence from the real world, which was saying a lot.

"Whatever are you up to, Marie?" he'd ask, intrigued, as she marched off with yet another handful of gears and scrap metal from his workshop.

"It's not ready yet," she'd always reply. "But soon."

Deep in the palace depths, down the longest staircase and safeguarded behind heavy iron doors, in a cavernous room surrounded by machinery, Marie worked. And worked. And worked. Until, finally, one day, she tightened the last bolt. She secured the last pulley. She adjusted the final lever, and focused the last lens.

"It's ready," she said, wiping her brow.

She stood back and admired her creation. A massive engine of grinding gears and pumping pistons. Water-powered turbines rotated, releasing steam that spun fan belts attached to pulleys that turned cogs that all connected to one giant glass-lensed tube pointed down at a platform in the center of the room.

A platform upon which sat Sugar Plum.

The machine was ready. It just needed the key.

Marie stepped up to a star-shaped keyhole in the side of

the engine. She withdrew her precious music box key from her pouch.

"Here we go," she whispered.

She inserted the key and turned it.

The engine wheezed. It whirred.

There was a bright flash of light.

CHAPTER 10

CLARA

Sugar Plum turned Clara's trinket box over in her hands. Her finger traced the six-pointed star keyhole, and a hopeful smile crossed her lips.

"I think it is," she answered. "Yes, it most definitely is *the* key!"

Hawthorn jumped up and down with glee. "The key! The key!" he cried. "Did you hear that, Shiver? At long last, we have the key!"

At Hawthorn's words, Shiver's expression suddenly clouded. "But we do not," he said, crestfallen. "It may be *the* key, but as young Clara said, it is lost."

Hawthorn's face fell as well. "Oh," he murmured.

"You lost it in the Fourth Realm?" Shiver turned to Clara. "To a mouse with a scar? That will be Mouserinks."

"The very same, sir." Phillip nodded.

Shiver passed a shaking hand across his face. "Ah, then Mother Ginger will have it, and all is lost."

"If I may be so bold," Phillip suggested, "we could mount an expedition, Your Excellency."

"I think that's an excellent idea," Clara chimed in, thankful for Phillip's steadfast resolve. "I must get that key back."

"We all must, my dear, we all must." Hawthorn leaned heavily against a pillar. "But you can't possibly go back to the Fourth Realm. It's a terrible place. It's pure fortune you got out alive."

"Hawthorn is right," Shiver added. "We cannot risk losing our princess when she has only just arrived."

"And, talking of arriving," Hawthorn continued, "where are our manners, regents? We need to organize a pageant to celebrate your coming."

"I think that's an excellent idea," Sugar Plum concurred.

"But the key—" Clara pressed. She could feel her chances at retrieving it slipping away.

"No, no." Shiver shook his head. "Out of the question."

Clara's face fell. She slumped down into one of the empty thrones.

"Uh . . . that's Mother Ginger's throne . . ." Phillip said nervously.

Sugar Plum swept to Clara's side and took her hand. "You have had a long, tiring day. Let me show you to your quarters."

Before Clara could protest, Sugar Plum escorted her out of the throne room. Clara cast a confused glance back to Phillip before the large double doors closed behind them.

"Mother Ginger has a throne?" Clara asked as they walked along a tapestry-lined hall. She didn't understand why such a horrible creature would have a dedicated seat in the palace.

"Mother Ginger used to be the Regent of the Fourth Realm," Sugar Plum explained. "Before she was banished."

"What happened?" Clara asked.

"When Marie . . . didn't come back," Sugar Plum said slowly, "Mother Ginger tried to take control of all the Realms by force. Your mother trusted us to guard the Realms in her absence. She trusted Mother Ginger. But Mother Ginger had other plans. She wanted to rule all your mother had created—on her own."

Sugar Plum guided Clara to a window overlooking the Fourth Realm. From here, Clara could see it was an island, shrouded in fog and fallen to ruin.

"These are frightening times," Sugar Plum said gravely. "We forced Mother Ginger into exile, but she created the monster that so nearly caught you and laid waste to the Fourth Realm."

She pointed to the drawbridge Clara and Phillip had ridden across upon entering the palace grounds. It was raised now, preventing unwanted enemies from the Fourth Realm from crossing over to the other three.

"That drawbridge won't keep out the mice much longer," Sugar Plum explained. "I don't think your mother would want you to go back to the Fourth Realm. I have a duty to keep you safe."

Clara stared out at the drawbridge. To think that it was all that was protecting her mother's greatest creation from complete ruin—she couldn't believe it. How could someone her mother had trusted have turned out to be so evil?

Sugar Plum gently took Clara's hand. "Come."

The beautiful regent led Clara through the palace corridors and up long staircases to a room tucked away high in a tower. Upon entering, Clara gasped.

"What a beautiful bedroom!" she exclaimed. The chamber truly was lovely, bedecked in satin and lace and flowers. A room fit for a queen.

"It was your mother's," Sugar Plum said. "And now yours, if you like."

Clara ran her fingers lightly over the soft, downy bedspread. A painting of her mother hung on the wall. Sugar Plum was in the painting next to her. The two girls appeared to be laughing, enjoying a sunlit afternoon in a field of flowers. Clara gazed at the painting for a long moment. Her mother looked younger in the picture. Happy, and full of life.

Clara felt the familiar tightness in her chest. It was as though her mother were all around her in the delicate beauty of the bedroom, close enough to speak to, to touch, but just beyond reach.

"Please, Sugar Plum," Clara said. "Tell me about my mother."

Sugar Plum smiled. "We went everywhere together," she said. "We were inseparable—skating on the riverbanks, dancing in the courtyard, taking candies off houses when no one was looking. We would stay up all night in the flower gardens, just talking and talking. Ah, such happy times."

The corners of Sugar Plum's lips dipped down as she spoke. Clara thought she must be filled with great sadness, realizing those memories could never be relived. Clara understood, because she felt the same way.

Suddenly, Sugar Plum looked to Clara. "Darling Clara, can you keep a secret?" she asked conspiratorially.

Clara nodded. Sugar Plum took her hand and led her

through another doorway, up a short flight of stairs, and into a room filled with machinery. Gears slowly turned, ticking by the seconds. Twelve windows with closed curtains lined the walls.

"Your mother and I treasured our jaunts into the other world," Sugar Plum said with a sly smile.

"The other world?" Clara asked.

"Your world," Sugar Plum replied.

She pulled back one curtain, revealing the crackled glass of a window with a large number printed backward. Through the blurry glass, Clara could just make out the view of Drosselmeyer's ballroom far below them, decorated in Christmas finery.

"It's Godfather's ballroom!" she cried. "We're in his clock! But—how?"

The machinery behind them suddenly began to whir more loudly. Something was about to happen.

"It's time," Sugar Plum urged. She hurried Clara to a moving platform. "Wait—wait—okay, now! Step up!"

Together, Clara and Sugar Plum hopped onto a moving platform powered by a conveyor belt that ran around the length of the clock room. It moved them swiftly toward a door, which opened in a burst of light, leading to . . .

"We're out!" Clara exclaimed as they rushed into the light and sound of the ballroom Christmas party. From their vantage point high up on the grandfather clock, Clara had a bird's-eye view of the entire festivity. But she was not her normal size— she was as tiny as a toy figurine. Clara looked down at her hands. She *was* a figurine! She and Sugar Plum had turned into miniature versions of themselves, moving along the outside of the grandfather clock on a tiny winding conveyor belt like two decorations ringing in the hour as the clock chimed. Clara gazed in wonder as the magic of the Realms shimmered around her.

"How is this possible?" she asked in disbelief.

Sugar Plum just smiled. "Your mother's favorite view. And mine."

Clara gazed in wonder at the joyful party beneath them.

"There's Father, Fritz, and Louise!" she cried suddenly. Clara pointed to her family standing in the center of the party. Fritz was playing with his nutcracker, trying to make their father laugh. Meanwhile, a handsome young man spoke with Louise.

"She's so lovely, isn't she?" Clara said of Louise, noticing again how much she resembled their mother in the beautiful green gown.

"Is she?" Sugar Plum asked, tilting her head. "Oh, yes, sweet. But don't forget, your mother chose you to come to the Four Realms. Not her."

Clara couldn't help feeling a flush of pride. Sugar Plum was right. Her mother *had* chosen her for this adventure. Even though she might not be graceful, or poised, or know the right thing to say at the right time, her mother had trusted her enough to share this wonderful secret. And that meant everything.

The conveyor belt rumbled along, bringing Clara and Sugar Plum around the length of the clock and leading to an automated door. Just before they passed through, Sugar Plum leaned closer and whispered in Clara's ear.

"I used to watch you growing up from here and wonder when your mother was going to bring you to meet us."

They burst through the door and back into the cool, dark room inside the clock.

"That's what she did." Clara grinned, holding up the precious egg. "She gave me this, and here I am!"

"At last," Sugar Plum agreed. "She was *so* clever!"

"But . . . won't my family worry where I've gone?" Clara suddenly realized.

"No, no," Sugar Plum assured her. "Time moves so slowly

there. You'll be back before they've noticed. If you really want to go back."

"I can't go back until I've found the key," Clara said, determined.

"I quite understand," said Sugar Plum. "But until then, you are the guest of honor at our pageant. All the citizens of our world will want to see you!"

Sugar Plum grasped Clara's hand once more and guided her back to her mother's lovely bedchamber. The beautiful regent rushed to a gilded wardrobe and threw open the doors. Rows and rows of gorgeous ball gowns hung on satin hangers.

"So, which one will you choose for your debut?" she asked.

At that, Clara hesitated. "I don't know," she said, uncertain. "I'm not very good at dresses and hair and shoes and, well . . ." Clara's voice trailed off. She knew the regents were only trying to welcome her. But she wasn't sure she wanted to be honored at a pageant where all eyes would be on her. Clara wasn't shy, but here, in the Realms, where her mother had been so revered and beloved and perfect . . . what if she didn't live up to their expectations? What if they were disappointed? Clara wished more than anything she could talk to her mother. She wanted the key so she could know her mother's final message.

Sugar Plum stepped up behind her. "If I may be so bold as to suggest that I help?"

"Would you?" Clara asked with relief.

"Of course!" Sugar Plum exclaimed. "It's my favorite thing."

A short while later, Clara sat in front of the vanity mirror, her eyes closed. Piles of dresses surrounded her, and Sugar Plum put the finishing touches on Clara's hair.

"No peeking," Sugar Plum reminded her. "You're almost ready."

Clara nodded. The way Sugar Plum lightly combed and pinned her hair was far more delicate than Louise's touch, but still not quite the same as her mother's.

"Did my mother ever talk about me?" Clara asked quietly.

"Oh, yes, all the time," Sugar Plum replied. The last pin she was placing accidentally poked Clara's head a bit too much, but Clara didn't mention it.

"So much so it sometimes seemed you were right here with us," Sugar Plum finished. "Now, open your eyes."

Clara did as she was told and stared at her reflection in the mirror. She gasped.

"Oh!"

Clara looked . . . magnificent! Sugar Plum had selected a stunning winter-white gown embellished with feathers and flowers for her to wear to the pageant. Gold brocade circled the bodice and arms, and her hair was intricately braided with shimmering ribbons and pearls.

Clara had never seen herself look so lovely. For a brief moment, she actually felt as beautiful as her mother.

"Do you like it?" Sugar Plum asked.

"I love it," Clara answered. "I look so . . . different."

Sugar Plum smiled. "Like the daughter of a queen."

A bright flash of light.

Then sound, and color, and a face.

"It worked!" the girl before her cried.

"What worked?" Sugar Plum asked.

"My machine," the girl answered. "You're real now."

"Am I?" Sugar Plum looked down at her hands. They were soft, smooth, and white.

"Yes," the girl said, drawing her into a hug. It was the most heartfelt, joyful hug Sugar Plum would ever know. "And you're perfect."

That had been Sugar Plum's first memory with Marie, back when it was just the two of them in the Realm. Now she had lots of memories! And the Realm wasn't just one realm any longer, but four, each filled with toys brought to life by Marie's clever invention—the Engine.

With the joyful discovery that the Engine was a success,

Marie and Sugar Plum had made dozens and dozens of friends to play with. China dolls, puppets, even miniature figurines all transformed into picture-perfect people, very happy and eager to explore their new home. And once there were so many citizens, they of course needed houses. And shops. And places to play and eat and enjoy themselves. So together, Sugar Plum, Marie, and all the citizens had figured out ways to use Marie's tinkering contraptions to build entirely new towns throughout the beautiful landscape. It was easy, really, once they got started. Simple contraptions Marie had built in the real world could be used in the Realms to create so many things.

A tinkered machine that blew puffs of steam would send clouds billowing up to the heavens.

An ordinary oven with a few mechanical tweaks and a "quick bake" button could whip up enough cookies to form sweet cobblestoned streets.

A tinkered garden plow could till acres of fields in minutes. A mechanically tweaked icebox could produce enough ice to form entire glaciers. And Sugar Plum's favorite—a prototype candy floss maker Marie said her uncle Drosselmeyer had brought back from his travels abroad—could make enough spun sugar to form into any shape imaginable, all while shimmering like glass.

Marie told Sugar Plum that everything she created had a special purpose or memory associated with it. And along with the new citizens, the two friends transformed the landscape of the Realm into the fairy tale wonderland of the Four Realms.

"Tell me the story again," Sugar Plum would often beg Marie as they gazed out the palace windows at the splendor stretching far to the horizon. "What does each of the realms mean?"

Marie would smile and hold her friend's hand as she pointed to each.

"The Land of Flowers." She gestured to a flower-filled valley bursting with color. "Like my father's garden outside his clock shop."

She directed Sugar Plum's attention to the mountains in the distance, where an ice cathedral sat nestled among frozen cottages and icy pathways. "The Land of Snowflakes," Marie explained, "to remind me of the day I came to Drosselmeyer's estate."

Sugar Plum leaned out the window to spy the realm in the opposite direction. Carnival rides peeked out from between the towering evergreen treetops: Ferris wheels, carousels, circus tents, and spinning towers. On the forest floor, grand banquet tables were set with tea party finery. "The Land of Amusement," Marie said, "for my mother."

"And our favorite realm?" Sugar Plum pressed eagerly, her eyes sparkling like sugar.

The two friends turned to view the candy-confection backdrop of the realm closest to the palace. It was a bustling town, vibrant with life and pastel color. Peppermint pathways crisscrossed between gingerbread houses, lollipop lampposts, and even a frosted-sugar fountain.

"The Land of Sweets," Marie replied, nudging her friend's shoulder. "To remind me of you."

Sugar Plum's cheeks would flush candy-floss pink with pride whenever Marie told her that. No matter how many unique citizens Marie brought to life with the Engine—jolly bakers and flower peddlers and even Christmas carolers who went door to door each day singing holiday tunes, whether it was Christmas or not—Sugar Plum always knew she was the most special of all. She had been first, and as Marie said, she was perfect.

Sugar Plum simply adored her friend's visits to the Realms. A few times, Marie had brought the old man Drosselmeyer with her as well. The first time he visited, he had seemed stunned upon seeing the splendor Marie and Sugar Plum had created together.

"Goodness, child!" he'd exclaimed. "How long have you been working in here?"

"A while," Marie had giggled. "But strangely, it doesn't feel like that long at all."

"Because she has us!" Sugar Plum had thrown her arms around her friend's shoulders. "We did it together. Marie is our queen!"

"Your queen?" Drosselmeyer asked, raising an eyebrow. "Marie, I had no idea royalty was something you fancied."

Marie had smiled sheepishly. "Well, with the palace and all, it seemed fitting."

"And rightfully so," Drosselmeyer conceded. "After all, this world is from your imagination. It only follows that you should watch over it." Drosselmeyer gazed around the spectacular landscape in amazement. "It is truly stunning. Your parents would have been proud."

Sugar Plum could tell Marie was pleased that the old man was impressed.

The only thing better than creating life in the Realms, in Sugar Plum's opinion, was playing in them. Whenever Marie was there, the two girls were inseparable, laughing and frolicking together from dawn until dusk.

On one such morning, very early, before the sun had even risen, Sugar Plum burst out through the grand palace's doors.

"Come along!" she shouted to Marie. "If you don't hurry, we'll miss it!"

"I'm coming!" Marie cried. Her ice skates banged against her shoulder as she hurried to keep up. She slipped and slid across the bridge all the way to the Land of Snowflakes. Meanwhile, Sugar Plum seemed to glide across as lightly as a feather.

"This way!" Sugar Plum urged her. "Hurry!"

The two girls passed through the tunnel leading to a thousand-step staircase that ascended all the way to the top of the Land of Snowflakes' frozen glacier. Marie panted for breath, matching Sugar Plum step for step.

"Why . . . are . . . there . . . so . . . many . . . stairs?" she huffed.

"Don't ask me," Sugar Plum called back. "You made it."

"Remind me to make a staircase with fewer stairs next time!" Marie laughed.

The girls climbed up, up, up, racing to make it to the top before they missed their chance.

"Almost there," Sugar Plum encouraged. "Quickly now!"

Thirty more steps . . . then twenty . . . then ten . . . until finally, the girls burst through the opening into the wintry realm at the very top. Glittery snowflakes collected on their hair and shoulders as they continued their speedy trek across the ice and snow. They ran up a high snowdrift and clamored over the crest before sliding down the other side, skidding onto a frozen pond at the base.

"We made it!" Marie breathed hard. "I didn't think we would."

"Just in time," Sugar Plum said. "Look up!"

She put her arm around Marie's shoulders and pointed to the sky. The first wisps of dawn were just breaking over the snowcapped mountains. Pink and orange streaked the horizon, but up above, where the edges of sunrise had not yet touched, misty swirls of yellow and green and purple began to dance across the heavens.

"They're beautiful," Sugar Plum whispered. "Tell me again what they are?"

"They're called the aurora borealis." Marie smiled proudly. "At least, that's what they're called in the real world. Colorful lights that appear because of magnetic charges in the sky far up in the north."

"And here?" Sugar Plum asked.

"Here, it's just . . . magic," Marie replied. "I've always wanted to see the northern lights since I read about them, but I didn't think it was possible. Then I realized anything is possible in here. With science, mechanics, and a little bit of imagination."

The two friends sat down on the fluffy snow. Sugar Plum leaned back against a snowbank. The glow from the colorful lights reflected on her porcelain white skin. "And with you," she said. "None of this would be possible without you." She hugged Marie tightly.

The girls watched in wonder as the lights continued to dance gently up above. Finally, the colors faded with the rising sun. The morning grew bright, and the green and orange and yellow vanished completely against the blue sky.

"Come on," Sugar Plum whispered. "Let's skate."

The girls giggled and laced up their ice skates. They pushed out onto the frozen pond, skating in perfect figure eights and practicing ballet leaps upon the ice. Marie fell often, but not Sugar Plum. Her movements were just as precise and delicate as when she'd been a windup toy.

Sugar Plum helped Marie up each time she stumbled and showed her the way to perform an arabesque while balancing on one skate. They whirled and twirled until, finally, their stomachs started to rumble—which meant it was time for their favorite treat: a visit to the Land of Sweets bakery.

Hand in hand, they bounced back down the thousand-step staircase and clamored along the peppermint cobblestoned streets. The scents of warm chocolate croissants and cinnamon donuts wafted through the air. Marie plucked two apple-walnut muffins from the bakery's tray and placed them in her basket while Sugar Plum poured steaming mugs of cocoa from a huge copper kettle. Then they skipped to the palace courtyard to enjoy their breakfast. They reclined on a tuft of green grass, chatting about how lovely the new flower vines looked, and how silly the tin soldier guards were, and wouldn't it be divine to go on a hot-air balloon ride over the Realms later that day?

"I love when we're together," Sugar Plum said happily. "I wish you could stay here all the time."

"Sometimes I wish so, too," Marie said.

Sugar Plum often wondered what it was like for Marie back in the real world. Did she have a beautiful bedroom there, too? As many fancy dresses as she did here? All the ginger biscuits she could eat? Sugar Plum didn't have any memory of her time in the real world. She'd only been a doll back then. But she liked it when Marie told stories of how she had played with her ever since she was a little girl. In a way, Sugar Plum felt like they had been best friends from the very beginning.

"How come you have to go back?" Sugar Plum asked. "Why not stay here, with me?" Her mouth was still full but she flashed a bright smile, trying to sweet-talk her idea. "We could play and skip and dance and do everything together all the time. It would never have to end!"

Marie laughed. "That would be grand." She took a sip of cocoa. "But I belong in the real world, too."

"Why? You're not a queen there." Sugar Plum playfully nudged her friend's shoulder. "But here, you are!"

"I know," Marie giggled. "But there are things I have to take care of in the real world. Lessons and schoolwork. And I made a promise to my uncle."

"What promise?" Sugar Plum asked.

"That I would always come back," Marie said.

"Oh." Sugar Plum thought about that for a moment. "Can you promise me, too?"

"Promise you what?" Marie asked.

"That you'll always come back," Sugar Plum said.

"Of course!" Marie hugged her tightly. "I'd never leave you."

Sugar Plum grinned wide, filled with happiness. She hopped

up, letting the apple muffin crumbs tumble from her lap onto the grass. "Race you to the flower fields!" she yelled.

"No fair!" Marie laughed when Sugar Plum sped off. "You always get a head start!"

The two girls bounded toward the Land of Flowers, their next adventure waiting just beyond the horizon.

And so it was every day in the Realms for Marie and Sugar Plum. Two best friends, like sisters, playing together without a care in the world.

One afternoon, in the Engine Room, Sugar Plum watched curiously as Marie held a new toy in her hands. The old man Drosselmeyer was with them. Whenever he came, something new or exciting was usually in store.

"It's magnificent, Uncle." Marie admired the handsome nutcracker doll Drosselmeyer had given her for her birthday. "Thank you so much."

"I'll admit, my gift is a bit self-serving," Drosselmeyer replied. "I'm eager to see your invention at work again."

"Of course!" Marie said. "He will make a perfect guard for the palace."

"Well, not *perfect*," Sugar Plum teased.

"Yes, of course." Marie touched noses with her. "Only you are *perfect*."

The girls laughed, having shared this particular joke many times before.

Marie placed the nutcracker upon the Engine platform. Then she hopped up to turn the star-shaped key on the enormous machine.

Whir. Click. Hummmmmmmmmmmmmm.

The machine buzzed to life, and with a bright flash, the nutcracker doll had vanished. In its place stood a real-life soldier, proud and tall, with rich brown skin and a brushed red velvet uniform.

The nutcracker soldier blinked. "Where am I?" he asked.

Marie placed a hand on his shoulder, as she did with each toy she brought to life. "You are home," she said. "My name is Marie. What's yours?"

The soldier gazed into Marie's eyes. "Phillip." He took an awkward step forward. Marie steadied him.

"Careful," she said. "Coming to life takes a bit of getting used to."

Sugar Plum watched the soldier regain his balance. Every time Marie brought a toy to life, their first steps were always so clumsy. But hers hadn't been. She prided herself on being as graceful as a ballerina from the start.

Meanwhile, Drosselmeyer reached out to touch the metal of the Engine. "I still can't believe it," he said to Marie. "Your machine uses nothing but steam power?"

"Yes. The turbines turn the conveyor belts that carry the different gears necessary to mechanize every toy," Marie explained. "Inside, they're assembled the way they would need to be arranged to allow the toy to move. But with the magic of the Realms, it does more than that. It brings them . . ."

"To life," Sugar Plum finished for her.

Drosselmeyer smiled proudly, like a father seeing his child accomplish a great task. "My dear Marie, only you could have thought of something so clever."

"She's brilliant, isn't she?" Sugar Plum took Marie's arm.

"I don't know about brilliant." Marie laughed. She gestured to Phillip. "Each toy that comes to life is unique in its own way."

"Perhaps I'm the magical toy that allowed the machine to work!" Sugar Plum suggested. "I was the first, after all."

"Maybe you're right," Marie said. "I would never have thought of the Engine in the first place if it weren't for you. You're my best friend."

That made Sugar Plum very happy.

"Which reminds me," Drosselmeyer suddenly announced. "Marie, your governess asked that we meet with her, together."

"She did?" Marie asked with a look of surprise. "Have I done something wrong?"

"No, no," Drosselmeyer assured her. "On the contrary, your studies are exemplary. But she is a bit concerned about your social exposure."

"'Social exposure'?" Sugar Plum repeated in a proper, stuffy voice. "That sounds ever so serious."

"What does she mean, Uncle?" Marie asked.

"I'm not entirely sure," Drosselmeyer replied. "But we shall find out together. Are you ready?"

"Of course, Uncle." Marie let go of Sugar Plum's arm. "I'll come with you now."

"But—" Sugar Plum started. She didn't want her friend to leave just yet. "I thought we were going to make snow angels. And then flower angels. And then candy angels."

Marie laughed. "We still can, silly. I'll come back as soon

as I'm finished. While I'm gone, why don't you show Phillip around? You can take him to the candy factory, or the flower gardens! The daylilies are all in bloom—your favorites!"

Sugar Plum watched as Drosselmeyer guided Marie out through the Engine Room door.

"She's always so busy," Sugar Plum mused to Phillip. "I wonder if people in the real world realize how clever she is."

"She must be very clever, to have invented such a thing." Phillip looked to the Engine. "Should we go to the candy factory, then? As Marie said?"

Sugar Plum shrugged. "I suppose so." She was honestly more interested in getting a head start on making lovely snow angels to surprise Marie when she returned. But then Sugar Plum glanced at Phillip's uniform and giggled. "Maybe they'll have some nuts for you to crack."

Phillip looked down at his hands and uniform and laughed as well. "I'm afraid I won't be much help with that anymore," he admitted.

The next year, Christmastime arrived again at Drosselmeyer's estate. And this was a very special year, Marie told Sugar Plum.

She had always asked her uncle for a party at Christmas, but this year, Drosselmeyer had taken it one step further. He was hosting a grand ball to celebrate—the first ever at his manor!

"Will you help me do my hair?" Marie begged Sugar Plum. "I can never make it look as lovely as you do."

If Sugar Plum could have, she would've glowed with happiness. "Of course!" she gushed. "I will make you look like royalty."

High in the palace bedroom tower, Sugar Plum worked hard to pin Marie's hair up just right. She coiled her friend's dark brown tresses into an intricate bun at the nape of her neck. Then she wove sprigs of holly and berries Marie had brought from the real world around her head like a Christmastime crown.

"It's gorgeous." Marie admired the stunning hairdo in her mirror. "Oh, Sugar Plum! What would I do without you?"

"Your hair would be tangles!" Sugar Plum teased.

Marie leaned in close, as though about to share a secret. "Come," she said. "Let's take a sneak peek at the party from the grandfather clock."

Together, they scampered up into the mechanized clock room and hopped onto the conveyor belt. In the blink of an eye, the belt whisked them outside and they stood as two delicate figurines upon the tall clock.

Not long ago, the two girls had discovered the grandfather clock portal would allow them to peek out at the real world as though they were two figurines belonging to the clock itself. Another mystery of the Realms discovered by chance. Afterward, Marie had asked her uncle to move the clock to his grand ballroom so that she and Sugar Plum could observe the annual Christmas party festivities from their secret vantage point. She knew that Sugar Plum would enjoy the revelry, even if she couldn't be there in person.

"Isn't it fantastic?" Marie asked, gazing upon the party below. "It's so cheerful. And lively! I've never seen so many people in one place."

"We should host a party in the Realms, too!" Sugar Plum exclaimed. "With all the citizens gathered at the palace."

"What a wonderful idea!" Marie clapped her hands. "We could have a tree and presents and . . . oh!"

Marie suddenly stopped. Her eyes fixated on a particular spot on the ballroom floor below. Sugar Plum followed her gaze.

Several children were dancing about the Christmas tree. They laughed and chattered as they spun.

"Children!" Marie gasped. "Uncle didn't say there would be *children* at the party. I thought it would be only grown-ups. But look! I know them! I've seen them in town—they're my age! Oh, what fun!"

"Do you really think so?" Sugar Plum pursed her lips. "I suppose they look . . . nice." Truthfully, Sugar Plum thought the children looked rather ordinary. Their clothes seemed simple, and their hair wasn't styled nearly as fancily as she had done up Marie's. Whatever dance they were doing looked quite silly, but perhaps that was how children in the real world played. Sugar Plum had never met any, besides Marie. So she really had no way of knowing.

"Uncle must have wanted to surprise me," Marie continued eagerly. "I should hurry down now, so I don't miss them."

"Oh—you're leaving so soon?" Sugar Plum asked, a bit disappointed. "I thought you were staying for a little while longer."

"But I—" Marie started. The conveyor belt clicked along, depositing them back in the main clock room. "I thought that was why you fixed my hair to look so lovely. So I could go to the party."

"It is!" Sugar Plum insisted. She struggled to find the right words to explain what she was feeling. "It's just . . . time moves so differently here. It feels like you're gone for ages when you leave. I wanted to play together a bit longer before you go. It's Christmas Eve."

Marie seemed surprised at her friend's confession. "It really feels like that long when I'm away?" she asked.

Sugar Plum nodded. "Can you please stay? Just for a bit. I promise, the children will still be at the ball when you get back."

Marie looked longingly out the blurry glass window to the ballroom below. The children were dancing a reel in slow motion.

Then she sighed and smiled at Sugar Plum. "I guess I can stay for a bit longer. I'm sorry—I knew the time moved differently here, but I never thought of how long it must feel for you while I'm away. What would you like to do? Oh! Perhaps we could play dress up! I could even make us a few new gowns with the tinkered sewing machine I brought from my uncle's workshop. We can have a ball gown gala!"

"What fun!" Sugar Plum clapped her hands. Inside, she felt a welling of relief that Marie had agreed to stay. "We shall look so lovely."

"Like sisters." Marie touched her nose to Sugar Plum's.

"Like queens," Sugar Plum agreed.

CHAPTER 12

CLARA

A trumpet blared, announcing the beginning of the pageant. Hundreds of citizens of the Realms were gathered in an enormous theater, seated before a grand stage. But all eyes were focused not on the stage, but on the balcony where Clara was seated alongside Sugar Plum and Phillip.

"On this momentous day in the history of the Four Realms," Shiver announced loudly, "we are proud to present before you Clara Stahlbaum, daughter of Queen Marie!"

An enormous cheer erupted from the crowd. Citizens waved in adoration, and parents held children up on their shoulders to get a better look at their princess.

Clara waved back, feeling a little overwhelmed. She was not used to having all the attention on her, much less the attention of an entire kingdom.

"What are they all staring at?" she whispered to Sugar Plum.

"You," Sugar Plum replied with a smile. "You are every inch your mother's daughter."

Clara felt a rush of pride.

The lights dimmed, and a hush fell over the crowd as the stage curtain rose. A lone ballerina dressed as a princess stepped gracefully out into the spotlight. She began to dance. Pirouettes, arabesques, attitudes. Her movements were lovely, but sad. The music sounded melancholy to Clara, as though the ballerina were all alone.

Sugar Plum leaned over. "The pageant tells the story of the Four Realms," she explained in a whisper. "How your mother created our world."

In the orchestra, a piccolo began playing a brighter tune, and the princess ballerina's steps quickened. Her bourrées turned into pirouettes. Her steps to jetés. The music swelled, and with the gentle crescendo of a cymbal, the stage filled with magical twinkles. The princess's expression changed from sorrow to joy as she raised her graceful arms toward the sky. Sparkling snowflakes drifted down from up above.

"The Land of Snowflakes," Sugar Plum whispered to Clara.

The ballerina kicked her foot. Colorful flowers sprouted from the ground.

"The Land of Flowers," Sugar Plum continued.

Then a backdrop of sweet treats unfurled from behind the dancing princess.

"The Land of Sweets!" Clara exclaimed.

The ballerina continued to leap and dance across the stage. With each kick and pirouette, more glorious embellishments sprang to life.

Then a chorus of dancers entered from the wings, all dressed as toys and dolls. Their costumes were mesmerizing: pink and gold delicately spun from flowers and sugar and crystals. But as lovely as they were, their movements were not. Windup keys protruded from their backs, and their dancing was stiff and mechanized.

"This is how we began," whispered Sugar Plum. "Lifeless toys."

Onstage, the princess ballerina swept over to one of the dancers. He was dressed in red and black: a robotic toy soldier. With one elegant movement, the ballerina whisked the windup key from his back. Instantly, his movements became graceful and fluid. He took the ballerina's hand, and together, they performed a delicate pas de deux.

Then the ballerina began removing the windup keys from

all the toys' backs! They sprang to life, dancing with joy as the music reached a rousing crescendo.

All at once, the music changed. Violins and flutes grew silent, and an ominous oboe tune echoed throughout the theater. A new dancer entered the stage. She walked upon tall stilts, her curly red hair hanging in strings about her face. She wore a big hoopskirt and a frightening mask. The other dancers cowered in fear.

"Mother Ginger?" Clara asked quietly.

"The one and only," Sugar Plum confirmed.

As the other dancers hid, only the princess remained unafraid. She approached the ghastly Mother Ginger and removed her windup key. Instantly, the horrible woman sprang to life. She knocked the beautiful princess to the ground! Tiny dancers dressed as mice scurried out from under her skirt, attacking the other dancers onstage!

"Was this the battle with Mother Ginger and the mice?" Clara asked.

"Yes." Sugar Plum nodded solemnly. "Beastly woman. There's nothing motherly about her. She began this war." Sugar Plum leaned in close to whisper in Clara's ear. "I hope you will be the one to finish it."

The beautiful princess ballerina escaped to the stage wings, and the toy dancers rallied in a valiant balletic war against Mother Ginger. Mice leaped this way and that, some being thrown into acrobatic leaps, others somersaulting over toys as they attacked. Fog overwhelmed the stage until only the dancers' outlines were visible. Then, with a brilliant trumpet fanfare, Mother Ginger and her evil mice retreated while the toy dancers onstage rejoiced. They were triumphant! The vile regent and her minions had been banished to the ruins of the Fourth Realm.

The crowd rose to its feet, cheering and applauding. Clara clapped as well, but she was confused by what Sugar Plum had told her.

"I don't understand," she said. "What do you mean, you hope I am the one who will finish it?"

Sugar Plum looked around. All the citizens, even Shiver and Hawthorn, were distracted with their applause. The dancers onstage bowed.

Sugar Plum glanced to Phillip and nodded.

"Come with me," she whispered to Clara.

CHAPTER 13
SUGAR PLUM

"Come with me!" Marie encouraged Sugar Plum one morning in the Realms. "I have a surprise for you!"

"A surprise?" Sugar Plum asked with, well, surprise.

"Yes!" Marie tugged her friend up the wide palace steps. "Something I made for you in the palace."

"But how?" Sugar Plum stumbled to keep up. It wasn't often Marie's steps outpaced her own. "Haven't we been together the whole time you've been in the Realms?"

Marie winked. "This was special. I wanted to keep it secret until it was ready."

They reached a large set of double doors Sugar Plum had never seen before, and Marie turned to her. "Close your eyes," she whispered. "Don't open them until I tell you to."

Sugar Plum did as she was told, and Marie guided her into the mysterious room.

"Okay," Marie said. "Now!"

Sugar Plum opened her eyes and gasped. They were standing in an enormous throne room, brand-new to the palace. Marie must have spent ages perfecting it. The walls were engraved with elaborate designs of gears and wheels shimmering in pure gold. Marble columns supported ornate buttresses and archways. The entire space was illuminated by candlelight, reflecting off thousands of tiny crystals strung from regal chandeliers. And precisely positioned before four floor-to-ceiling windows were four stately thrones, each facing outward to overlook one of the realms.

"What is this?" Sugar Plum asked with wonder. "What have you made?"

"Can't you tell?" Marie asked excitedly. "It's a throne room!"

"For me?" Sugar Plum was confused. "But why? You are our queen."

"Because," Marie said, clapping her hands, "you deserve something special and grand! A room fit for royalty!"

Sugar Plum's cheeks flushed pink with pleasure. Was Marie planning to make her a queen, too, so they could rule the Realms together? Sugar Plum had never thought of herself as a queen. But now that she had, oh, it did sound marvelous!

"How lovely!" she exclaimed to Marie. "I can't believe—"

Suddenly, she paused.

"But why are there four thrones?" she asked.

That was when Sugar Plum noticed three other figures in the room with them. New toys brought to life that she had never seen before. They were each seated upon one of the thrones facing outward, and to Sugar Plum, they looked . . . different.

"You can come out now!" Marie called to them. "Come and meet Sugar Plum!"

"Oh, finally!" the first one said, bounding down from his throne. He was jolly and round, cloaked in robes made entirely from vibrant flowers. Even his hair sprouted roses.

"Hawthorn, at your service," he said to Sugar Plum, taking her hand and shaking it vigorously. "A pleasure, a *pleasure* to meet you."

"I'm—charmed, I'm sure," Sugar Plum sputtered.

The second figure came up to greet her. "Shiver," he said, introducing himself with a deep bow, allowing his silver dress coat to skim the floor. Wherever it touched, ice crystals formed. "It's an honor to meet you, Sugar Plum. Marie has told us so much about you."

"She has?" Sugar Plum asked. What was happening? Who *were* these people?

Finally, the last figure approached. This one was a woman,

dressed in a frilly orange-and-burgundy gown edged with tassels like ornate draperies. Her curly red hair puffed all about her head, tied up with yellow ribbon.

"And I am Mother Ginger," the woman announced. Her voice sounded older, more direct. "It's so wonderful to meet you, dear. You are as lovely as Marie told us."

Sugar Plum looked from the three of them back to Marie.

"I'm—I'm afraid I don't understand," she said.

"These are our new friends!" Marie explained. "I made them so you can be regents of the four different realms!"

"Regents?" Sugar Plum asked.

Marie took Sugar Plum's hands. She looked practically aglow with excitement. "I've been thinking for some time—you helped me make the Realms come to life, and I want you to lead it with me. But I'm not able to come as often as I used to, and it seemed so unfair to ask you to rule the entire Realms on your own. So I made you three companions. It's perfect, you see!"

Marie turned to Hawthorn.

"Hawthorn is the Regent of the Land of Flowers. He's a master gardener, just like my father was."

Hawthorn's cheeks blushed rosy red. "Oh, come, come, now. Surely I couldn't hope to be as masterful as your father!"

"You are every inch," Marie said with a smile. She turned to Shiver. "Shiver is the Regent of the Land of Snowflakes."

"Which reminds you of the day you arrived at Drosselmeyer's estate." Shiver nodded, pleased. "I am so eager to meet this Mr. Drosselmeyer whom you made me in honor of."

"And you will soon, I promise!" said Marie. She turned to the woman with red hair.

"And Mother Ginger is the Regent of the Land of Amusement. I thought of the name Ginger because my mother always used to make me ginger biscuits for my tea parties. They were my favorites."

"And mine, too," Mother Ginger replied warmly.

Marie leaned in close to Sugar Plum. "Do you know what that makes you?" she asked.

Sugar Plum opened her mouth, but no sound came out. For one of the first times in her life, she was speechless.

"It makes you the Regent of the Land of Sweets!" Marie cried, hugging her friend and jumping up and down. "Isn't it perfect? Oh, Sugar Plum, you're going to be so happy. We're going to have a pageant and a ball and everything! It's a new chapter for the Realms, with you at the very center!"

Sugar Plum's mind raced as Marie jostled her about. She

wanted so badly to be as happy as her dear friend. But none of this made sense.

"I still don't understand," she said slowly. "You won't be our queen anymore?"

"Oh, no! No, no, no. I will still be your queen," Marie assured her. "It's just, with my starting at the academy this fall, I won't be able to come to the Realms as often, and I—"

"Academy?" Sugar Plum interjected. "You're going to an academy? But why?"

Marie laughed. "To learn, of course. Everyone goes to an academy. Well, perhaps not everyone. But everyone does go to school. So they can learn and work and teach a family of their own one day."

"Oh." Sugar Plum thought about that for a long moment.

"Don't—don't you like your surprise?" Marie mistook Sugar Plum's hesitation for disapproval. "Aren't you pleased? Oh, please say you like it, Sugar Plum. I thought of it all for you!"

"Of course I like it." Sugar Plum didn't want to disappoint her friend. "It's all just very . . . overwhelming."

"You'll love it, you'll see." Marie hugged her again tightly. "You'll be so beautiful as the Regent of the Land of Sweets."

"Beautiful indeed!" Hawthorn chimed in. "The fairest regent

in the Realms!" He clapped a hand over his mouth. "No offense, of course, Mother Ginger."

Mother Ginger raised an eyebrow. "None taken, my dear man."

Relieved, Hawthorn continued. "It will be great fun! The Four Realms will be in good hands with us."

"Hawthorn is correct." Shiver touched Sugar Plum's arm. His fingers felt like ice. "Together, we four must look after the Realms while our queen is away."

"And so we shall." Mother Ginger stepped forward and took Marie's hands in her own. "We will be happy to care for the Realms in your absence."

Sugar Plum gazed at the three new regents. They did look friendly, she supposed. It would take some getting used to. But if this was truly what Marie felt was best, surely she could make it work. After all, she was the first. Perfect, like Marie always said. How hard could it be to teach three new regents the intricacies of caring for the Realms?

Mother Ginger seemed to feel Sugar Plum's eyes upon her. The woman turned and flashed an odd smile.

Sugar Plum quickly looked away.

She would try her best.

CHAPTER 14

CLARA

Sugar Plum led Clara and Phillip down a winding stair-case. The cheers and applause of the theater audience faded behind them as they went down and down, until all they could hear was their own soft footsteps upon the stone. Gas lamps flickered on the walls, causing their shadows to dance.

At the very bottom, they reached a heavy iron door. Sugar Plum suddenly gripped Clara's arm.

"You mustn't tell anyone I've shown you this," she whispered urgently.

Clara nodded. "I promise."

"Your mother wasn't just our queen," Sugar Plum explained in a hushed undertone. "She was also our creator. She made us."

Clara frowned. "I don't understand."

"Once we were mere toys," Sugar Plum continued. "Lifeless playthings for little children like yourself. Then your mother came and changed everything. She gave us life. With this."

Sugar Plum pushed the heavy door open, its hinges groaning in protest. Beyond was a cavernous room filled with machinery. Clara had never seen anything like it before. Stepping through the doorway was like stepping into the inner workings of a vast machine. But it was all strangely quiet. Pistons and cogs stood at the ready; fan belts and pulleys remained uncharacteristically motionless. The only things that moved were a series of water-wheels, turning very slowly. And at the heart of it all was a long, tapered tube pointed down at a platform. The machine hissed with steam, waiting for someone, something to activate it.

"The Engine," Sugar Plum said.

Clara gazed about the room, her eyes wide. "This is my mother's invention?" she asked in disbelief. Clara knew full well how talented her mother had been at tinkering. But the mechanism before them was so complex, clearly so powerful. Clara had no idea her mother was so ingenious an inventor as to have created . . . *this*.

"The Engine made us real." Sugar Plum ran her pale white hand along the smooth metal of the machine. "Gave us life and humanity. Everything that you have, we have. Feelings— happiness, sadness, anger—"

"Love," Phillip suddenly interjected.

Clara and Sugar Plum both looked at him in surprise. Embarrassed, Phillip patted a bit of metal on the machine. It released a valve, hissing steam at him. He coughed.

"Oh, yes, sweet captain, certainly love," Sugar Plum acknowledged. "But we don't have the one thing we need to make it work anymore."

"The key," Clara said.

"As you see." Sugar Plum pointed to a huge pile of discarded keys lying by the control panel. "Without the key, the Engine lies dormant—the Realms are at a standstill. Mother Ginger is on the march and the mice are getting in. What happened in the Fourth Realm could happen here. Everything your mother created could be destroyed."

"No!" Clara exclaimed. "That can't happen."

Clara studied the keyhole that operated the marvelous Engine. She withdrew the egg-shaped trinket box from her pouch and gazed at its keyhole. They matched.

"It's the same!" Clara realized. "My mother couldn't return, so she sent me to give you the key!"

Maybe that is the message inside the box! Clara thought wildly. *Maybe Mother knew the Realms were in danger, and she sent me to save them. The note did say "Everything you need is inside."* Could she have meant *everything I need to save the Realms?*

"We waited and waited for your mother to return so we could start the Engine again," Sugar Plum said gravely. "But alas, she never did return. And now I very much fear the key has gone forever."

"No! We can get it back. We *must* get it back," Clara insisted.

Sugar Plum shook her head. "It is strictly against protocol to go against the wishes of the regents."

"But what about my mother's wishes?" Clara urged.

That gave Sugar Plum pause. "A good point, my sweet," she said after a long moment. "A very good point."

Clara and Phillip watched anxiously as Sugar Plum seemed to mull over Clara's words. Finally, the beautiful regent smiled. Her pink cheeks shimmered in the misty steam from the Engine.

"Then protocol be dashed!" she declared.

"Oh, thank you, Sugar Plum!" Clara hugged her, delighted. "Phillip?"

The soldier clicked his heels, at attention. "Your Majesty?"

"Will you come with me?" Clara asked. "To the Fourth Realm?"

Phillip nodded. "A dozen of my best men will be assembled

in the courtyard at dawn. We'll be in and out, mission complete by nightfall."

Clara grinned broadly. They were going to do it! They were going to get her mother's key back!

But Sugar Plum still looked concerned. "Clara, are you really willing to risk your life for us?"

Clara nodded, determined. "We must get the key. For all our sakes."

At that, Sugar Plum took Clara's face in her hands. Her touch was gentle, yet firm. Her skin was cool as marble against Clara's cheeks.

"You have her courage, too," Sugar Plum said with admiration. "How proud she would have been of her brave daughter."

An overwhelming feeling of gratitude washed over Clara.

Just a short while ago, she hadn't even known any of this existed.

But now, it was up to them—to her—to save it. To do what her mother would have wanted to, but no longer could. To keep her dream alive.

They were going to save the Four Realms.

Clara and Phillip stood before the drawbridge. Behind them were a dozen of his bravest soldiers, all at the ready. And in front of them, across the bridge, lay their destination: the destroyed Fourth Realm, shrouded in fog and uncertainty.

"I wish I could come with you," Sugar Plum whispered to Clara. "You understand I can't be seen to go against the other regents."

Clara nodded. She proudly wore a soldier's uniform for their mission.

"I understand," she told Sugar Plum.

"But I have an emissary to assist you in your search," Sugar Plum continued. "A fine navigator whom I trust with my life."

Sugar Plum looked around. "Dew Drop?" she called.

"Oh, no," Phillip groaned as a tiny fairy flitted over to them in a crackling trail of sparks.

"Did you say something?" Dew Drop asked, squirting him with a magical spritz of water. "Couldn't quite catch that."

"How beautiful!" Clara exclaimed. She had never seen a real fairy before!

Dew Drop landed upon her shoulder. She studied Clara's face.

"Which is more than I can say for you," she quipped.

"I beg your pardon?" Clara asked in surprise.

"Dew Drop," Sugar Plum warned, "behave."

"What?" Dew Drop complained. "I thought she would be taller!"

Sugar Plum shook her head and turned to Clara and Phillip. Even in the dim early-morning light, the beautiful regent's porcelain skin shimmered like stardust.

"I pray for your safe return," she told Clara. "Take care, and beware of Mother Ginger."

"I will," Clara promised.

CHAPTER 15

SUGAR PLUM

O ver time, Sugar Plum grew used to the presence of the other three regents. Five years had passed since Marie began her studies at the academy in London. Her visits to the Realms had indeed grown much less frequent, though Sugar Plum alone seemed to feel the full impact of her dear friend's absence. It was never quite the same as the old days when it had just been Sugar Plum and Marie. But the regents' company made the stretches between Marie's visits a little less lonely, and every so often, Sugar Plum would forget for the briefest of moments that they hadn't been there all along, watching over the Realms with her.

In fact, Sugar Plum was pleasantly surprised by what a natural leader she made. She quite enjoyed her newfound prestige. The workers in the Land of Sweets readily did what she asked, building new peppermint pathways, laying out lavish banquets of sugary confections, even repainting her and Marie's favorite bakery to match Sugar Plum's own lovely colors. And they were happy to do so! Every request was met with a cheerful smile and delight at being able to please their beautiful regent. Sugar Plum fancied she must be a natural leader to be so loved.

The other regents performed their duties with similar decorum. Hawthorn was a bit bumbling, Sugar Plum thought, but he did have a magic touch with flowers. Fresh buds appeared beneath his footsteps whenever he walked outside. And though he was incessantly excitable, he treated Sugar Plum with the highest regard. He even created a flower just for her—a cross between a petunia and a plum blossom he called the Sugar Plum Petunia. Sugar Plum had been so honored she'd requested bouquets of her special flower to be delivered to her chambers every morning.

Shiver, she found, was more reserved. He'd watch over his realm from his throne for hours, gazing out at the frozen landscape, lost in thought. Every so often, he'd point a finger toward the horizon and redirect a snow cloud to sprinkle a different section with fresh flurries. But for the most part he remained quiet and pensive—except for that time he went skating with the children and fell through a hole in the ice. Then he had prattled on *at length* about the indignity. It had taken hours to chip away the excess icicles so as not to accidentally chip off parts of his frozen hair and beard. Sugar Plum had been tickled pink by the silliness of the incident for a whole week.

The only regent she never felt comfortable around was Mother Ginger. The old woman was innocuous enough. She kept to her business, minding the games and festivals in the Land of Amusement, though Sugar Plum could hardly remember a time she'd seen Mother Ginger appear even remotely amused. But the one thing Sugar Plum couldn't *stand* was the woman's attitude whenever Marie visited the Realms. While Sugar Plum was elated to have her best friend back, even if for a few hours, Mother Ginger always seemed eager for Marie to return to her life in the real world.

"Don't you have studies you should be attending to?" Mother Ginger would ask. Or "What new inventions have you been working on? Surely they require your complete attention." And the worst was when she'd press Marie about suitors. "Has anyone captured your heart yet?" Mother Ginger would badger over and over again. "A lovely young woman such as yourself should not walk through life alone."

"She's not alone." Sugar Plum always stepped in to defend Marie. "She has us. And the Realms. How can a queen ever be alone?"

Mother Ginger would just shake her head in disapproval. Sugar Plum couldn't help wondering—why was Mother Ginger asking so many questions about Marie's life in the real world? What could possibly be so interesting about it to the old woman that she was always eager to send Marie back there as quickly as possible?

Yet, deep down, Sugar Plum knew there was a kernel of truth to Mother Ginger's words. Marie *had* grown into a lovely young woman. Even when she wasn't dressed in regal finery, an aura seemed to glow about her. Her very presence was uplifting, kind, and generous. If the citizens of the Realms adored Marie so, what did the people in the real world think?

"What's it like there?" Sugar Plum asked one evening, as Marie was about to begin her long trek down the wooded corridor. "In the real world?"

"It's lovely," Marie replied. She pondered for a moment. "More concrete, I suppose. More serious. Being here, in the Realms, I feel limitless. But when I'm there, I feel like . . . like I'm working toward something. An end."

Sugar Plum gazed down the long corridor. Was that a tiny flicker of lamplight at the very end?

"Can I go with you?" she asked. "I'd like to see what it's like."

Marie shook her head. "I don't think you can," she admitted regretfully.

"But we go outside on the grandfather clock," Sugar Plum pointed out. "To see the ballroom."

"That's different," Marie said slowly. "I think when we're looking through the grandfather clock portal, we're actually part of the grandfather clock. The magic of the Realms protects us. But going out into the hallway, it's different. We tried to bring something back once, long ago. It didn't work. Things made in the Realms couldn't exist outside in the real world. I think you would return to being a doll."

"A doll?" Sugar Plum said with distaste. "Oh."

Marie touched her friend's cheek. "Your place is here," she reassured her. "Where it's sweet and perfect. The real world can be confusing sometimes. You belong here, where it's always happy."

Sugar Plum placed her own hand over Marie's. "I'm happier when you're with me," she confessed. "I feel . . . different. I miss the old days, when we used to play together as sisters."

Concern crossed Marie's face. "Aren't you happy with the other regents? I thought you would be. I made them to keep you company."

"Oh, they do," Sugar Plum mused. "In their own ways, I suppose. But they're not you. They're not my family."

"Your family?" Marie repeated.

"Yes." Sugar Plum nodded. "It's like you said—we've been together since the beginning. Even before the Realms. Even before Drosselmeyer's estate."

A faraway look came to Marie's eyes. "It feels like so long ago," she whispered. "A different life."

A chime echoed somewhere in the distance. Perhaps it was even the grandfather clock, tolling from Drosselmeyer's ballroom.

Marie looked down the corridor and then took Sugar Plum's hands. "I must go now. But I promise, I'll be back soon. It's nearly Christmas! And we'll have a grand celebration, just like the parties in Uncle's estate." She winked. "Perhaps I can even think of a surprise, for old time's sake."

Christmas Eve arrived. Snow fell gently outside the palace windows, blanketing all the Four Realms in wintertime serenity. Marie had returned, just as she'd vowed. She was dressed in a rich green-and-gold ball gown, ready to attend her uncle Drosselmeyer's Christmas celebration.

But now, she had gathered all the regents in the throne room with the promise of a very special surprise.

Sugar Plum glowed with anticipation. Christmas Eve was always such a magical time, the evening she looked forward to the most. Not because of the tree or the snow or even the presents, but because she always knew that on this night, out of every other night, Marie was guaranteed to come back to them.

And though Marie didn't know it yet, Sugar Plum had an extraordinary surprise in store for her dear, dear friend as well.

"I have presents!" Marie exclaimed to the gathered regents, her smile warm and cheeks rosy. "Special gifts I designed just for you."

She handed each regent a beautifully wrapped present.

Hawthorn opened his with relish. "Seeds!" he cried, holding up a vial filled with tiny rainbow-striped flower seeds.

"Not just any seeds," Marie said. "Exotic seeds my uncle Drosselmeyer brought back from his travels to the distant tropics. These flowers cannot grow in the cool England air. But here, in the Realms, I thought—"

"It will be an honor!" Hawthorn exclaimed. "I shall tend to them myself in their own dedicated field in the Land of Flowers. They shall grow lovelier than any other flower here in the Realms!"

Marie grinned. "I knew you would be excited," she said.

Shiver went next. He carefully unwrapped his gift, revealing a delicate glass pocket watch. The case shimmered like ice, and the interior workings of the tiny clock were visible through the clear glass, clicking and whirring away.

"I made it myself," Marie explained. "The glass reminded me of ice. I can't work with ice in the real world. But I wanted to give you something that still felt as magical as—"

"The Land of Snowflakes," Shiver finished. A tiny frozen tear formed at the corner of his eye. "It's beautiful, My Queen. Thank you, thank you. I shall treasure it forever."

Mother Ginger looked to Marie. "Is it my turn, dear?" she asked.

"Yes," Marie answered. "Please."

Mother Ginger opened her box, glitter from its delicate brocade wrapping floating to the ground. Inside was an ornate wooden nesting doll. Mother Ginger gently opened it to reveal another doll nestled within, and inside that was another, and then another—five dolls in total, each smaller than the last. The larger dolls were painted as a mother and father, and the smaller ones as children, a boy and a girl. The last was a baby.

"I found them in a trinket store," Marie explained. "I don't know why, but they made me think of you. They're so pretty. Something my mother would have loved. Do you like them?"

For one of the first times Sugar Plum could remember, she saw Mother Ginger's expression soften.

"I do," she said, clearly touched. "Thank you."

Last was Sugar Plum. The beautiful regent turned her gift over in her hands. Tiny pinpricks were poked into the sides of her present.

"Open it," Marie encouraged her. "Go on."

Sugar Plum lifted the lid. In a flurry of glitter and sparks, a tiny creature flew out!

"Oh, my!" Sugar Plum gasped. "A fairy!"

"Not just any fairy!" the tiny fairy piped up. "The sweetest fairy of them all! Dew Drop's the name."

"Do you recognize her?" Marie asked Sugar Plum.

Sugar Plum looked more closely at the fairy. The fairy looked closely back at her.

"Is she . . . the hair clip I made for you?" Sugar Plum asked. "Out of crystallized sugar?"

Marie nodded and clapped her hands. "The very same. It took some very fine tinkering, but I was able to find gears minuscule enough to use with the Engine to bring her to life. I thought she would be the perfect companion for you—a tiny friend that we each had a part in making. Like family."

A feeling Sugar Plum hadn't felt in a very long time spread through her. Like the warmth she remembered from Marie's very first hug, or the joy she'd felt as they watched the aurora borealis together. A feeling of peace and love.

"She's perfect," Sugar Plum breathed. "I love her."

Dew Drop landed lightly on Sugar Plum's shoulder. She tilted her head. "'Love's' a strong word there, Pinky. We've only just met. Let's get to know one another first."

Sugar Plum raised her eyebrows and looked to Marie.

Marie shrugged. "She turned out a bit . . . saucy. But I thought maybe, with your graceful touch—"

"Don't worry, Queen Bee." Dew Drop fluttered over and patted Marie's cheek. "I'm sure Sugar Plum Bun and I will get along just fine."

"We have a present for you, as well, Your Majesty," Shiver announced. "A royal pageant, the first of its kind."

"It tells the story of how you created the Realms!" Sugar Plum burst in, unable to contain her excitement any longer. "It's a beautiful ballet—I choreographed it myself. You'll be *so* impressed! It has waltzing flowers and falling snowflakes and everything! It's positively *perfect*. A pageant fit for a queen. But first, we've prepared a wonderful banquet in your honor. With all your favorite Christmas treats! Hot cocoa and spiced oranges and ginger biscuits. Come! The food will be ready!"

Sugar Plum leaped up and tugged on Marie's arm, but Marie remained seated.

"Oh, my darlings," she said. "I wish I could. But I promised Uncle Drosselmeyer—"

"No!" Sugar Plum interrupted without thinking. "Not tonight. It's Christmas Eve!"

The other regents looked at Sugar Plum in surprise.

"Sugar Plum, I'm—I'm so sorry," Marie stammered. "But . . . Uncle's party has already begun. There's someone he wants me to meet—a young man named Charles. He's the nephew of a dear family friend, and Uncle was just about to introduce me when I begged him to let me come here to give you your gifts. He said I could, if it was just for a few minutes. If I stay much longer, I will appear rude. I must go."

"But—" Sugar Plum felt all the previous joy and warmth drain out of her. In its place seeped the cold, bitter sting of disappointment.

"Of course, you must go, child." Mother Ginger stepped in. "You mustn't keep your uncle waiting."

"She's not a child!" Sugar Plum snapped. "She's our queen."

"And our queen has duties to attend to," Mother Ginger countered. "She created us to guard the Realms in her absence. That is what we will do. Even on Christmas Eve."

"I—" Marie seemed torn. "I'm so—"

"It's all right, Your Majesty," Shiver spoke. "Mother Ginger is right. Your time is precious, and we are honored you came to spend these moments with us. We are most grateful for your generous gifts."

"They're really quite extraordinary!" Hawthorn bubbled. "I'm sure we can reschedule the pageant upon your return. Can't we, Sugar Plum?"

Everyone looked to the Sweets Regent. Sugar Plum didn't speak.

She had worked hard on this pageant for Marie. Unimaginably hard. She had spent hours teaching the ballerinas the dance moves herself, never accepting anything less than perfection. There were times she'd even driven them to rehearse through the night until the sun shone brightly over the Realms and the dancers could barely keep their eyes open for want of sleep. She'd perfected every tune, handcrafted every costume using the very tinkered sewing machine Marie had brought to the Realms all those years ago. Because on this night, of all nights, Sugar Plum wanted to remind Marie of how magical the Realms were. How much the citizens loved and needed their queen.

But as the regents stared at her, wide-eyed and critical—and as Marie gazed sadly toward the palace doors, already one foot in the direction of home—Sugar Plum could feel her entire plan crumbling to pieces. Everything she had looked forward to, gone before it had even had a chance to succeed.

"Sugar Plum?" Hawthorn repeated. "We can reschedule, can't we?"

In a daze, Sugar Plum clenched her jaw and nodded.

"It'll be fine, Pinky!" Dew Drop flew up to Sugar Plum's hair and sat cross-legged in her pink coif. "Now did someone say spiced oranges? I like my treats spicy."

"I'll come back soon," Marie vowed. "I—"

"Promise," Sugar Plum finished for her. "I know."

The regents bid farewell to their queen. But as soon as Marie left, Sugar Plum raced away. Tears streaked her cheeks like syrup.

Why does Marie always have to leave? she thought sadly. *Why do we always come second? Who is so important in the real world that they're more important than we are on Christmas Eve? Than I am?*

Sugar Plum dashed up the tallest tower, taking the steps two at a time with graceful ballet leaps. She flew through Marie's bedchamber and pushed past the door leading into the grandfather clock room. With a grand sweep, she threw open the curtains and pressed her face against the blurry window. Her warm tears made little steam clouds against the glass as she gazed down to the ballroom below.

Marie had arrived back at the celebration. In slow motion, Drosselmeyer guided her over to the Christmas tree. The handsome young man named Charles stood there, tall and dapper. Sugar Plum's heart sank as Marie took the man's hand. Even in slow motion, she could see Marie blush.

"You cannot stop time," Mother Ginger's voice echoed behind her.

Sugar Plum wheeled around. The old woman stood in the doorway. She walked up beside Sugar Plum and followed her gaze out the window.

"That is why we are here," Mother Ginger said. "Marie can't stay with us forever."

"That's not true," Sugar Plum insisted tearfully.

Charles and Marie walked to the dance floor. Their steps took an eternity.

"But we can still make the Realms perfect," Mother Ginger continued as though Sugar Plum hadn't spoken. "On our own."

"It is already perfect," Sugar Plum muttered. "As long as it has Marie."

Mother Ginger shook her head. Below, Marie and Charles began to dance.

"All young ladies must grow up."

CHAPTER 16

MARIE

"It's beautiful, darling. As only you could make it."

Charles placed a loving arm about his wife's shoulders. Side by side, they admired the Christmas tree in their festively bedecked parlor. It stood lovely and tall, the pièce de résistance of Marie's holiday décor expertise with its shimmering glass ornaments, crimson velvet bows, and even candied pears and sugar plums.

Marie leaned against Charles, bouncing a chubby baby boy in her arms. Despite having been married for nearly a decade, she still adored the way her husband lit up whenever she revealed the hard work she had done to bring the Christmas spirit alive in their home. It was always as though he were seeing it all for the first time through the eyes of a young child.

"How do you make something so simple appear so magical every year?" Charles asked.

Marie smiled. "It's not magic," she replied. "Just imagination."

The baby reached eagerly toward a shiny ornament, and Marie gently backed him away.

"Ah, ah, Fritz," she tsked. "You're much too little for those." She nuzzled his cheek, making the baby laugh. Though he was barely a year old, crumbs from his first taste of ginger biscuit stuck like paste around his lips.

Suddenly, the parlor doors burst open. Six-year-old Clara and eight-year-old Louise bounded into the room.

"Mother! Father!" Clara shouted. "Is it Christmas yet? Is it?"

A strand of shiny metal bits connected by a string dangled from her hand. They clattered across the parlor floor as she hurried toward the Christmas tree.

"Almost, my darling little mechanic!" Marie handed baby Fritz to Charles and swept Clara up in a hug. "Now, what tinkering present have you brought me?"

"I made Father Christmas's sleigh!" Clara held up her handiwork. The bits hanging along the string were not bits at all, but rather tiny reindeer assembled out of gears and wire. At the end was a paper sleigh with a miniature red cushion attached for Santa to sit on. It wasn't perfect, but for a six-year-old, it was pretty clever.

"How lovely!" Marie exclaimed. "Father Christmas will be very pleased."

It warmed Marie's heart to see Clara taking such an interest in tinkering. Both her daughters made her so proud.

Louise had inherited Charles's quiet confidence and strength—the very traits Marie had fallen in love with all those years ago. Friends of the family often remarked how Louise carried herself with impressive grace for a child her age. Marie marveled how her firstborn was already turning into a proper young lady. Sometimes, she would secretly observe Louise playing with her dolls and tea set from around the corner. Her daughter never let a single drop of tea spill or a tiny crumb fall. Marie even had to stifle giggles when Louise instructed her stuffed animals on the finer points of *manners*. If only a stuffed bear *could* watch where it stepped with its muddy paw prints, that would be something indeed.

But Clara—her precious little Clara—she had inherited Marie's mechanical ingenuity. Marie recognized the spark right away when, at just three years old, Clara had grabbed her father's gleaming pocket watch from the table and pointedly asked, "How does it work?" Now that Clara was older, Marie had started to introduce her to basic tinkering concepts. But she would need to move her to more complicated lessons soon. Clara would not be content tinkering model Santa sleighs for long.

And when the time is right, Marie thought happily, *I will show Clara the Realms. Not yet. But one day.*

Marie touched noses with Clara, and the little girl giggled.

"Clara, that sleigh is too small for Father Christmas." Louise sat upon the sofa and smoothed her dress. "He won't fit."

"It's just pretend." Clara rolled her eyes. "But Father Christmas is magic. Maybe he *could* fit."

"He's still as big as us," Louise pointed out.

"Then how does he fit down the chimney?" Clara stuck out her tongue.

"Never mind, my dears." Charles laughed. "I'm sure Father Christmas will fit just as well in both his sleigh *and* the chimney tonight. Now come! It's Christmas Eve. And your mother and I have a surprise for you. One gift to open each before heading to Godfather Drosselmeyer's party."

"Hooray!" Clara and Louise cheered, forgetting all about gears and chimneys and disagreements.

The family sat together in front of the tree, skirts and legs crisscrossing upon the carpet.

"I'm so glad we can give them this," Marie whispered to her husband as the girls began opening their presents. "It means the world to them. And me."

"Did your parents let you open one present on Christmas Eve when you were little?" Charles asked.

Marie rested her head on his shoulder. "I wish I could remember." The memories from her life before the fire were distant and fuzzy, the details scattered away by time. "I do remember the feeling, though. The love. And I've always wanted this. A family of our very own to share Christmas Eve with. You've made my dreams come true."

Charles kissed her lightly on the head. "We did it together," he said.

Clara suddenly bounced back into her mother's lap. She held a windup toy she'd just opened, and Marie could see her clever darling was already peeking inside the tiny apparatus to determine how it worked.

Marie hugged Clara close, breathing in the soft scent of her hair.

"That we did," she whispered to Charles.

Heaps of mechanical bits and bobs lay scattered about Drosselmeyer's workshop. Marie watched eagerly as Clara, now twelve years old, crouched in front of an open control panel and tinkered away inside an enormous mechanical cylinder. The entire apparatus was perched atop a large circular platform with life-sized animal figurines stationed around the perimeter. Clara was up to her elbows in wires and gears, clinking and clacking her tools away.

"It's not working," Clara declared with aggravation. "I can't figure it out."

"Do not give up, my clever mechanic," Marie encouraged.

"You've made it too hard this time," Clara insisted. "I can barely figure out which wires I'm working with, let alone reconfigure them. They're tangled like a rat's nest."

"There's a way to figure it out," Marie assured her. "There's always a way."

Drosselmeyer was with them, observing Clara's efforts alongside Marie. "Perhaps if you reverse the mechanism . . ." he suggested helpfully.

"Shush!" Marie hushed him. "Don't give her hints."

Drosselmeyer shrugged. "I seem to remember a young

mechanic who would get rather frustrated when I wouldn't give her hints."

"She'll get it," Marie said with confidence. "She's my clever girl, after all."

Meanwhile, Clara grunted as she forced a stubborn screw to twist loose from deep inside the contraption. It clattered to the ground, and she quickly scrambled to nab it and place it securely in her tool pouch. Then she carefully selected two wires, one red and one blue, from the tangled labyrinth of electrical cables and switched their positioning. With a twist of her screwdriver, she secured them back into place and leaned back to wipe her brow, accidentally streaking oil across her forehead as she did so.

"That might do the trick," she said thoughtfully. "Do you think so, Mother?"

"There's only one way to find out," Marie said. "Turn the handle."

Clara reached for a crank handle on the side of the cylinder, and with a visible deep breath, forced it round and round.

Sparks flew inside the cylinder. A grinding rumble echoed beneath the platform. And then, slowly, the circular platform began to turn. The animals bobbed up and down, some spiraling in place, and warbly carnival music began to play.

It was a perfect carousel—not quite as large as one that could be found at a fair, but big enough to accommodate a handful of riders.

"It worked!" Clara clapped her hands. "I did it!"

"I knew you could!" Marie jumped up onto the carousel base and whirled her around, never minding the oil that streaked from her daughter's hands onto her own pretty dress.

"Well done!" Drosselmeyer nodded in approval. "Well done indeed."

"Godfather's hint did help," Clara admitted.

"Nonsense," Marie said. "I saw you tinkering with the wires in there. You knew you could reverse whatever mischief I'd done. Everything you needed was inside."

"Inside the control panel?" Clara asked. "Of course. I just wasn't sure how to reconfigure the wires to get it started."

"No, my darling." Marie tapped Clara's forehead, leaving a messy fingerprint upon her lovely daughter's brow. "In here. Everything you needed was right in here."

Clara beamed. Marie could tell her daughter was very, very proud.

Then Clara returned her attention to the smoothly rotating

carousel. "What shall we do with it? It's too large to stay in Godfather's workshop."

"As I have been saying for many months now." Drosselmeyer chuckled. "You two young ladies have taken over my workshop with your lessons."

The hint of a smile crossed Marie's lips.

"I think I might have a place for it," she said.

"Where?" Clara asked.

"Ah." Marie shook her head. "You'll have to trust me. That is a lesson for another day."

"Do you remember what it was like back then?"

Sugar Plum asked Marie the question late one night in the Realms. They were seated on the snowy banks of the frozen skating pond, looking up at the distant stars. The citizens of the Land of Snowflakes had long since retired to bed. But just for tonight, Marie wanted to stay awake as long as possible. To make up for lost time.

"Yes," Marie replied. "I remember the excitement—like magic the moment I stepped through the passageway. You were always there to meet me."

Sugar Plum listened, but didn't respond.

It had been a very, very long time since Marie had visited the Realms. Too long, Marie realized. She hadn't meant for so much time to slip away since her last visit, but with her husband and the children and her tinkering lessons for Clara . . . the days had a way of flying by before she'd even realized they'd gone. She knew it wasn't fair to leave Sugar Plum for so long without any explanation. So as a special surprise, she'd planned a full day to spend with her while Uncle Drosselmeyer watched the children. She and Sugar Plum could go ice-skating or race through the flower fields or bake gingersnaps—anything Sugar Plum wished, really. Drosselmeyer had promised to cover for Marie while she was away, should anyone notice her absence.

But Sugar Plum seemed . . . different, Marie thought. Distant, as though a mask covered her fair features and Marie couldn't quite see beyond it.

"What do you remember most?" Marie asked her. "From the old days."

Sugar Plum shrugged. "Not very much," she said.

"Really?" Marie asked, hurt.

"It's been a long time since then," Sugar Plum replied. "It's hard to remember that far back."

Awkward silence fell between them. Marie was at a loss for what to say.

"Has . . . all been well with the regents?" she finally asked.

"I suppose," Sugar Plum said. "Well, except for Mother Ginger."

Marie frowned. "What do you mean?"

"She's always wandering around the palace rather than minding her *Land of Amusement*." The words were tinged with sarcasm as Sugar Plum spoke. "Never a day goes by where she isn't polishing your crown."

"Oh," Marie started, "I—I may have asked her to do that once. She had a way of making it sparkle that I couldn't. It was just a silly request. I had no idea she still was doing it."

Marie looked to Sugar Plum, but her friend's gaze remained directed toward the stars.

"I can ask her to stop, if you like," Marie said.

Sugar Plum shrugged again. "It's not that important. I just assumed she fancied trying it on when no one was looking."

Marie opened her mouth to reply, but she couldn't find the

words. She had hoped for a long while now that Sugar Plum would grow closer with the other regents, and that she would start a life intertwined with them and all the citizens of the Realms. That was why she had made the regents and Dew Drop in the first place: to be there for Sugar Plum when she wasn't. The regents were the same as Sugar Plum, after all: ageless, all brought to life by the Engine. Marie *did* age, and she wouldn't be there forever. But surely Sugar Plum must know that.

"Sugar Plum," she started hesitantly, "there's something I've been meaning to talk—"

"Take me with you," Sugar Plum said suddenly.

"Where?" Marie replied. "We can go anywhere you wish. This is your special day."

"To the real world," Sugar Plum said, pressing. "I want to go back with you. You're always there and never here, and I want to be where you are."

Marie shook her head. "You know I can't."

"There must be some way," Sugar Plum insisted. "An Engine you could build in the real world. I was the magic toy that made the Engine work in the first place. Maybe it could happen again! Surely you could think of something?"

Marie wanted very badly to make her friend happy. But what she was asking for was impossible. "I don't know how," she said. "And I don't know what would happen to you."

"Do you not want me there?" Sugar Plum whispered.

"Oh, no!" Marie exclaimed. "I wish very much I could bring you back with me. The children would so love to meet you."

At that, Sugar Plum's expression changed.

"Would they?" she asked.

"Oh, yes," Marie declared. "Especially Clara. I see so much of myself in her. She's very clever. I think you two would be very good friends."

Sugar Plum didn't reply. Marie could tell her friend was upset. She didn't want it to be this way. This was their special time together. She wanted it to be happy, like old times!

"Maybe," she said slowly, "I could *try* to invent something. A machine to bring you back. I don't know how I'd do it. I can't guarantee it's even possible. But perhaps—"

Unexpectedly, Marie coughed, her words catching in her throat. She coughed again. Before she knew what was happening, a terrible fit overwhelmed her. She held one hand to her mouth and the other to her chest as she doubled over on the ice, unable to catch her breath.

"What's wrong?" Sugar Plum asked anxiously. "What's happening?"

"I'm—all right—" Marie gasped. "I—" Her ribs hurt.

Sugar Plum held her shoulders, trying to steady her. "I'll get you some water!" A moment later, she held an ice cup to Marie's lips.

"Drink this," she urged.

Marie did so. The cold water numbed her throat and spread down through her chest. After several more sips, the worst of the coughing subsided.

"Thank you." Marie regained her composure. "Sometimes I just start coughing so badly. I don't know why."

"I've never seen you like that," Sugar Plum said with urgency. For a moment, the hard mask was lifted, and Sugar Plum's face was the one Marie remembered. Kind and attentive, but clouded with fear.

"I'm sure I'll be all right," Marie assured her. "It will pass."

"I do remember the old days," Sugar Plum said hurriedly. "I remember everything, from the moment you made me. Oh, Marie, tell me your promise. Say it again."

"Promise?" Marie asked, confused.

"That you will always come back," Sugar Plum urged. "Promise you will always return, no matter what."

"I—" Marie started.

"Please!" Sugar Plum said, desperate.

Marie looked at her friend's face. The lingering pain from her coughing fit ached in her chest.

"I promise."

CHAPTER 17

CLARA

Phillip clicked his heels, and his soldiers snapped to attention. The drawbridge began to lower. Wisps of foggy mist rolled along the divide, spilling onto the palace grounds.

Sugar Plum lightly touched Clara on the arm. "Mother Ginger fooled us once before with her devious ways," she whispered in her ear. "Don't let her deceive you now."

The drawbridge locked into place with a resounding *thunk*, and just like that, the chasm dividing the Fourth Realm from the rest was sealed. Clara took a deep breath. There was no going back now. Their mission was under way. She had to be brave—they must succeed. For her mother.

The troops began marching across the bridge. As soon as their feet touched the land of the Fourth Realm, fog enveloped them, masking both vision and footsteps alike. But still, they marched forward, resolute. It wasn't long before they reached the forest's edge. Foreboding trees loomed tall, many with rotting, barren branches hanging at odd angles. Pine trees were clustered tightly together, the needles packed so densely anything could be hiding in there unseen. Just waiting to jump out.

Some of the soldiers began whispering nervously to one another.

"This way. Mush, mush! Hurry up!" Dew Drop heckled them, flitting this way and that in the mist.

"Stand firm," Phillip encouraged his troops.

A sudden gust *whooshed* past ominously. Dew Drop tumbled in the air, flung off course.

"Dangerous flying conditions, these," she muttered. "I might just return to base."

"You will do no such thing," Phillip instructed her. "This will not be like the last four times where you decided you'd rather have tea and biscuits than complete your task."

"Please, stay with us," Clara pleaded. "We need you."

Dew Drop scoffed. "Needy, yes? Isn't that always the way with princesses? 'My hair, my dress, my—'"

"Key," Clara interjected. "That's all I need. My key."

"As does everyone in the Realms." Phillip shot Dew Drop a pointed look. "Including you."

A distant rumbling noise suddenly came from under their

feet. Clara couldn't be certain, but she thought she felt the ground move.

"Did you hear that?" Phillip whispered.

Everyone listened in dreadful silence. Faint squeaks echoed from . . . somewhere. But in the thickening fog, it was nearly impossible to see what was around them.

Three soldiers beside Clara whispered in fear. Whatever terrifying stories they had heard about Mother Ginger and her mice had worked in the old woman's favor. Their resolve was wavering. Clara couldn't let that happen—she and Phillip couldn't do this alone. They had to keep the soldiers strong.

"Hold these out in front of you." Clara ignited several torches and began passing them out to the shaky platoon. "Mice don't like fire."

"Are you sure you want to continue?" Phillip whispered to Clara.

"I'm not leaving the Fourth Realm until I have that key in my hand," she replied. "So where you go, I go."

Suddenly, there was a muffled cry in the darkness. Clara wheeled around. Hadn't there been three soldiers beside her? Now there were only two.

"I'm sure we're nearly there," she said unsteadily.

Another cry echoed to their right.

"What's happening?" Clara asked.

"Stay together, men," Phillip ordered. "Tight formation."

The thick, rolling fog parted suddenly, allowing a shaft of moonlight to pierce through to the ground. It shone upon something in the darkness—a ghastly monster with sharp white teeth that glinted in the soldiers' torchlight!

"There's something there!" Clara cried.

"Stand back, Your Majesty!" one of the soldiers shouted. He thrust his sword at the menacing creature—a direct hit in its fiendish yellow eye!

But strangely, the creature didn't howl or blink. It didn't even move.

Clara cautiously reached out. In the flickering torchlight, she caught sight of the creature's scales, wings, and long pointy tail. And then . . . chipped paint? A pole running right through it?

"A carousel ride?" she asked.

The soldiers held their torches high. Sure enough, they were standing before a dilapidated carousel, overgrown with vines and roots. Carved swans, tigers, and dragons lay strewn about in the fog, pieces chipped off and limbs missing. The carousel's lamps had long since gone out, its controls covered with rust and grime.

I know this carousel, Clara thought, a rush of memory flooding back. *It's the carousel I worked on in Godfather's workshop . . . the one Mother tested me with!*

Clara had always wondered what her mother had done with the carousel when it finally disappeared from Drosselmeyer's workshop. She assumed that her godfather had helped Marie move it to a basement somewhere in the estate. Or that they had even sold it to a carnival.

But it's so large, Clara marveled. *How on earth . . . ?*

Then her mother's words came back to her. *I think I might have a place for it,* her mother had said. *That is a lesson for another day.*

The Realms, Clara realized. *She brought it to the Realms and made it full-sized. And she wanted to show me how she did it one day. Together.*

Clara gazed sadly at the mechanical masterpiece fallen to ruins. Her heart broke a little to see it in pieces. Broke a little for the lesson she would never share with her mother.

Who would have thought?

The ground rumbled beneath them again, and everyone instinctively clambered aboard the base of the carousel. Clara saw Phillip do a quick head count.

"We're missing four men," he said. "We'll never find them in this fog."

Clara glanced at the controls. They were just the same as she remembered. "Maybe we can guide them to us."

She quickly picked her way over broken shards of ceramic and glass and began rooting around in the rusty mechanism. She dug out two frayed wires. *Perfect,* she thought. *All it needs is a spark.* She touched them together and called to Phillip.

"Turn that handle!" She pointed to the large crank handle protruding from the carousel's center column.

Phillip did as she asked. As he cranked, a spark flew from the wires in Clara's hands. Instantly, the carousel's lights flashed to life, and the soldiers were able to get their first proper look at what remained of the Fourth Realm.

All around them lay a wasteland of broken life-sized toys, rusting and abandoned. The skeleton of a Ferris wheel leaned crooked against a tree, a steam engine toppled on its side at the base. Shattered remnants of tea party china and splintered tables were heaped about. Carriages were upended, their wheels missing. It was like a forgotten battleground of children's toys.

Clara stared, aghast. "What happened here?"

"Mother Ginger," Phillip replied grimly.

The ground shook yet again, only this time the rumbles seemed to be getting closer. Then, with a terrifying lurch, the carousel began sinking.

"Run!" Phillip cried to his soldiers.

The troops scattered in the fog, racing between the trees and tripping over crumbling toy remains. Holes began opening up everywhere in the ground. The unmistakable squeak of a thousand mice shrieked up from the depths.

"The mice are making sinkholes!" Phillip realized. "Everyone watch your step!"

But it was too late. One by one, soldiers disappeared beneath the surface. As soon as they'd dodge one hole, another would open up directly in front of them.

Clara looked around in horror. Their whole team was vanishing.

They had to get to safety and regroup!

Clara ran straight for a tall tree, ready to climb. But before she could reach it, an enormous sinkhole opened before her. She leaped over it . . . only to have a second hole immediately open where she was about to land!

"No!" Clara screamed.

"Clara!" Phillip cried, realizing what was about to happen. He skidded to a stop at the edge of the hole and reached wildly for her hand. He grabbed it just in time!

"Hang on!" he shouted.

Clara looked down. Her feet dangled helplessly above an infinite black abyss.

"I can't—" she cried. "I can't hold on!"

Clara's hand slipped . . . and she fell.

"Clara!" Phillip screamed after her as she tumbled down, down, down into the unknown. She scratched wildly at the hole's dirt walls, desperately trying to slow her descent. Her hands scraped against sharp rocks and tangled roots. But nothing eased her fall until, finally, she landed with a thud on what felt like a soft carpet upon the ground.

Clara looked down. She screamed in revulsion.

The "carpet" was actually a sea of wretched, furry mice. They crawled up and over her legs and arms, clawing at her hair!

"Get off me!" she screamed. "Get off!"

The mice lurched beneath her, carrying her on the wave of their furry backs down the earthen tunnel. The motion continued, sweeping her along another corridor and up toward the surface before—

Whoomp!

The mice flung her out into the foggy air, back above the surface. She rolled along the cold, hard ground, breathing heavily. Inexplicably, the mice scampered down off her arms and hair and scattered into the shadows. All at once, Clara was completely alone.

She stood up uncertainly.

"Phillip?" she called. "Dew Drop!"

"So, young lady!" a voice thundered high above her head.

The fog cleared, revealing a massive marionette towering over Clara. Its twisted face was curled into a hideous smile, its skirt as wide as a circus tent.

Mother Ginger, Clara realized with a cold feeling in the pit of her stomach.

The fearsome creature scooped Clara up in its palm, bringing her to eye level.

"You dare to come to my realm?" it boomed. "Just who do you think you are?"

Clara knew she should be frightened, but something about facing off with the sinister Mother Ginger—being eye to eye with the creature who had destroyed part of her mother's creation and threatened the rest—made her angry. She squared her shoulders, staying strong. She had to think of the key, and the Realms.

And her mother.

"I am Clara Stahlbaum," she proclaimed.

"Is that so?" Mother Ginger's voice echoed. It came from the marionette, but its lips never moved, remaining ever twisted into a grotesque smile.

"Yes," Clara declared. "And I have come to reclaim what you have taken from me and from my mother. My key."

Mother Ginger laughed, a force so terrifying Clara lost her balance in the marionette's palm.

"I'm not scared of you!" Clara shouted. "You're just a doll!"

At that, the entire marionette began to quake. Before Clara knew what was happening, the hand holding her *whooshed* down and swept Clara under Mother Ginger's skirt! She tumbled head over heels, somersaulting to a stop in the dusty earth.

She coughed and raised her head. Layers upon layers of tattered tulle made up the inside of Mother Ginger's skirt, eerily colorful compared to the bleak desolation of the Fourth Realm.

And then, something emerged from the tulle.

A clown with two gleaming yellow eyes.

CHAPTER 18
MARIE

"I need to ask you a favor."

Marie leaned heavily against Mother Ginger's throne in the palace. More time had passed—far, far too much time. Marie's children had grown lovely and strong: two smart young ladies and a mischievous little boy. But while time had strengthened her darlings, it had only seemed to make her weaker. She had tried to plan her visits to the Realms when her constitution was at its best. But those small windows of renewed health seemed to be ever smaller. Now, standing in the throne room, she clutched a stained handkerchief to her mouth.

"I'm happy to do anything you wish, Your Majesty," Mother Ginger replied. "But if I may ask, why aren't the other regents here?"

"Because I wanted to speak with just you," Marie said. "I—" She coughed, a violent racking that shook her whole frame.

"You're not well, dear." Mother Ginger placed a steadying

hand on her shoulder. "Perhaps you should return home to your—"

"No, I'm all right," Marie insisted. She pushed the handkerchief into her dress pocket. "But . . . the truth is, I may not be able to visit the Realms for a while. I'm . . . not as strong as I once was. The doctors have instructed me to rest. Which means it may be some time before I'm able to come again."

"Of course," Mother Ginger said.

There was a long pause.

Marie looked up. The red-haired regent was staring oddly at her. It was then Marie realized she hadn't made eye contact for the whole conversation—she'd been staring down at the floor, practically slumped in Mother Ginger's throne.

"Is it serious?" Mother Ginger finally asked.

Marie nodded. "Alas, there are some things tools can't fix."

"But you will recover?" Mother Ginger pressed.

Now Marie made every effort to stand up a bit straighter. "Yes, of course." She suppressed a cough. "With time. I just need time. But, as you know, a long time at home . . ."

"Is an eternity here," Mother Ginger finished for her. Her eyes suddenly flashed in thought. "Have you told Sugar Plum?"

Marie shook her head. "Not yet. I don't want to worry her."

"Then that is the favor." Mother Ginger nodded. "To tell Sugar Plum."

"Oh, no," Marie shook her head. "Not at all. I will tell her. Just not today—not while I'm looking so unwell." Her expression clouded for a moment, then she regained her focus. "I was hoping you could help take more of an active role in leading the Realms."

Mother Ginger's eyes flashed again.

"You mean rule?"

"Not exactly," Marie clarified. "I mean work together with the others."

"I do not understand." Mother Ginger frowned. "We already work together, don't we?"

Marie finally gave in and slumped upon the throne. She held her head in her hand; it ached so badly. "I've wanted for a long time for Sugar Plum to grow closer with the three of you. For you to all work together to watch over the Realms. When I created the Realms, I was just a girl. I never thought about the responsibility—of being a queen. I just wanted to create beauty, and imagination, and hope. The Realms are limitless. But I realize now that I've made more than I can promise to look after. The Realms shouldn't have just one leader. They were never meant to."

She looked up to Mother Ginger. The woman stood very still.

"I made the four of you regents because I knew I could trust you," Marie said. "To work together, as a family. You're each a part of me. And while I'm . . . recovering . . . I would feel very much relieved to know you were all working together to keep the Realms safe."

"I understand," Mother Ginger replied.

"I would have asked the others here as well," Marie said. "But you remind me so much of my mother. I felt I should tell you first. I fear seeing me like this will cause the others great concern."

Mother Ginger drew Marie against her, comforting her as a mother would. She patted her head.

"Do not worry, my dear."

She gazed out the windows at each of the Four Realms, starting with the Land of Amusement, scanning across the flower fields and frozen glacier before resting her sights on the Land of Sweets.

"I will take good care of everything."

CHAPTER 19

CLARA

The round-bodied clown leered at Clara, its yellow eyes unsettling. Mad.

Then a seam opened up along its middle, revealing a second smaller clown within. The second clown popped out, and the first rezipped its seam with a horrible scratching noise. The second clown did the same, and more and more round-bellied creatures appeared, tinier each time, tumbling out like Russian nesting dolls.

They cartwheeled around Clara, laughing.

Polichinelles.

Clara backed away instinctively, but there was nowhere to escape. They had her surrounded.

The clowns tightened their formation, closing in around her. Then they attacked! One flipped over her head, smacking her shoulder. She stumbled out from their circle, but another tumbled into her, shoving her back into their trap. The Polichinelles quickly overwhelmed her with acrobatic attacks. They babbled and chortled as they soared—the maniacal laughter Clara and Phillip had heard when she'd first arrived in the Realms.

"Yi dong ta! Pasado! Ey ya zdes podprygivayu!"

Clara ducked as a Polichinelle leaped toward her, only to be tripped up by another cartwheeling at her feet. A third somersaulted straight into her stomach. Clara toppled to the ground, winded.

From her vantage point on the dirty, dusty ground, she suddenly noticed something she hadn't spotted before: ropes were draped about the center of the floor, all leading up to the torso of the gigantic marionette. And in the center of Mother Ginger's enormous skirt was a pole with a spiral cut into it, like a screw. A small seat was attached at the base. Someone—or something—was using those ropes to operate the marionette!

"You're no monster!" Clara exclaimed as the Polichinelles lined up for another attack. "Someone's controlling you!"

Thinking fast, Clara feinted left and dodged the flying Polichinelles before diving right and tripping up two more. That bought her just enough time.

She hopped onto the seat and pulled a nearby lever. Then

she shut her eyes as the seat shot up into the torso of the doll, spiraling the whole way.

The seat spun to an abrupt stop, leaving Clara dizzy and nauseated. But she regained her composure quickly, looking around. She was now in the torso of the marionette doll, in what appeared to be a large control room. Levers and knobs were planted about the walls, meant to operate the marionette's movements.

And dangling high above the center of the room, attached to a golden string, was the key.

Her key.

Clara reached for it. Her fingers had almost brushed the edge when a voice rattled her.

"Hands off, girl!"

She spun around. Standing behind her was an elderly woman with curly red hair tousled loosely about her face. She wore a burgundy velvet dress hemmed with gold brocade. The woman stared hard at her, not vicious, but imposing. Like a figure of great importance.

"You're Mother Ginger?" Clara asked.

"And you're Queen Marie's daughter, apparently," the old

woman replied. "Tell me, what business has Queen Marie's daughter got in the Fourth Realm?"

Clara squared her shoulders. "I've come to get what belongs to me. That key."

Without hesitation, Clara reached for the key. But the old woman was fast. She pulled one of the marionette's levers, causing the whole doll to tilt. Clara stumbled backward, hands empty.

"Ah, ah." Mother Ginger clicked her tongue. "Now that's not true, is it? If that key belongs to anyone, it's your mother."

"It opens the trinket box she left to me," Clara declared. "After she passed away."

A momentary flicker of doubt seemed to cross Mother Ginger's expression.

"Marie's dead?" she asked.

Clara nodded.

Mother Ginger's eyes drifted away for the briefest moment. "I didn't know."

"As if you care!" Clara shot back. "You're trying to destroy everything my mother created!"

A bitter smile curled at the corners of Mother Ginger's lips. "Oh, yes, that's what sweet Sugar Plum has been telling you?"

"I can see for myself," Clara snapped. "The Fourth Realm is destroyed, thanks to you."

"But you're seeing through sugar-coated eyes," Mother Ginger replied. "What if I were to tell you that your mother's key unlocks more things than just a little trinket box? What if I were to tell you what actually happened after your mother left us to rule ourselves?"

For a moment, Clara hesitated.

Then Sugar Plum's words echoed in her head. *Don't let her deceive you now.*

"Why should I believe you?" Clara said.

"You don't have to." Mother Ginger stepped toward her. "But why not listen anyway?" Another step. "Then decide what to do with the key." One step more. "Decide how the story ends, hmm?"

Mother Ginger was close enough to touch Clara. But before she could, Clara yanked one of the levers. The entire doll tipped, sending Mother Ginger sprawling back upon the control panel. The key swung toward Clara, and she grabbed it.

"No! Clara, wait!" Mother Ginger pleaded. "Please!"

But Clara wouldn't listen. She leaped onto the chair and pressed the release button. *Whoosh.* With a final look into

Mother Ginger's piercing eyes, she spiraled down, down, down, all the way to the floor of the enormous marionette.

To her surprise—and delight—Phillip was there. And he had successfully subdued the Polichinelles!

"Clara!" he exclaimed. "This way!"

Her brave friend led her out through a slit he had carved in Mother Ginger's enormous skirt. They ran as fast as their legs would carry them, leaping over mouseholes and plunging forward through the darkness.

"Are you all right?" Phillip shouted to Clara as they bolted.

"Fine!" Clara leaped over a large hole. "But Mother Ginger was . . . different." Clara couldn't shake the look she'd seen in the old woman's eyes as she'd spiraled down the pole chair. Not fury or malevolence, but . . .

Fear, she realized. Mother Ginger's eyes had been filled with fear.

"Don't be fooled by that little old lady act," Phillip warned. "She's deadly."

Suddenly, Mother Ginger's voice echoed through the darkness. "After them, mice!"

"See?" Phillip shouted.

Together, Clara and Phillip raced through the forest,

crashing through branches and underbrush, Clara clutching the key at all times. Finally, they reached the tree line, bursting through to the fog-patched plains leading back to the bridge. The glory of the other three Realms stretched out before them in the distance. They had made it. They were out of the fog—out from the Fourth Realm. And they had the key.

Dew Drop suddenly flitted about Phillip's shoulder.

"About time!" she exclaimed. "Were you having a tea party in there?"

"There's no time for your antics," Phillip snapped. "We have the key. But Mother Ginger won't be held off for long."

"What about the other soldiers?" Clara asked, worried. "We can't just leave them."

"Dew Drop, you're the navigator." Phillip looked to the fairy. "Guide them out, and be quick. Mother Ginger's not far behind us."

"All right, all right," Dew Drop agreed. "But keep hold of that key, you hear?"

She buzzed off into the mist, a trail of sparks fizzling out behind her.

Still partially winded, Clara wandered over to the cliff's

edge, overlooking the rushing water in the chasm far below. She sat down.

"We should return to the palace," Phillip urged. "It's not safe here."

"Just one moment," Clara insisted. She withdrew the trinket box from her pouch and held up the golden key.

This was it. The moment she had been waiting for. The moment she had braved mice and marionettes and great danger to reach.

She was finally going to know her mother's last message. Perhaps it would help her save the Realms.

Clara held her breath and inserted the key into the egg's lock. Her hand shook as she turned it. The key clicked.

Barely breathing, she opened the dainty contraption.

A lovely melody began tinkling out.

"A music box?" Clara blinked in confusion. "I don't understand. I thought . . ."

Suddenly, Clara felt the familiar tightness in her chest. The egg wasn't playing just anything. It was her mother's melody—her favorite song. The one the string quartet had played at her godfather's ball.

The one her father had wanted to dance to.

Clara stared inside the music box, turning it over in her hands.

It was empty. Nothing more than the music box mechanism surrounded by tiny mirrored walls within. She looked in every crevice, around every gear. But there was nothing. No message. No memory.

Nothing.

What did it all mean? Had the message been lost? Taken?

Or perhaps, Clara shuddered, tears forming at the thought, *perhaps there was never a message to begin with.* Perhaps she had misunderstood her mother's note. Perhaps she had been wrong all along.

Clara closed the music box, bringing its melody to a halt.

"What's wrong?" Phillip knelt down beside her.

"My mother told me everything I needed was inside," Clara said sadly. "But it's empty."

Phillip reached over and grasped the music box. He opened it, causing the tinkling melody to play again.

"Close it, please," Clara insisted.

"Why?" Phillip asked, confused.

"It was my mother's favorite tune," Clara said.

She looked to Phillip. He still seemed confused.

"It reminds me of her," Clara explained. "And how much I miss her. It hurts."

"Oh," Phillip said. "I've never had anyone to miss."

Clara's shoulders sagged. To have come all this way . . . to have discovered so much about her mother she hadn't known . . . only to find there was no message waiting for her at the end after all.

"I thought there would be something inside," she admitted to Phillip. "Something beautiful, personal, useful—anything. But I came all this way for nothing. It makes no sense."

"For nothing?" Phillip raised an eyebrow. "You did what no one else here could. You found the key. The key that can save us all."

Clara thought about that. "Yes, I guess that's true."

"And at the same time, you've proved that you're fearless, strong, and loyal." Phillip picked up Clara's soldier hat, dusted it off, and handed it to her. "There's some sense in that."

Clara smiled. "Thank you, Phillip," she said, grateful.

For the most fleeting of moments, no words passed between

them. Only the rising sun's light filtering between the clouds.

Then Phillip nudged her.

"Come on, soldier girl," he said. "We have to go save the Realms."

CHAPTER 20

MARIE

Drosselmeyer hurried down the ballroom steps, taking them two at a time. He couldn't believe his eyes.

"Marie, whatever are you doing here?"

Marie staggered up the base of the stairs. Her coughs echoed through the entire hall. In a heartbeat, Drosselmeyer was at her side, guiding her toward a nearby chair.

"You shouldn't be out of bed," Drosselmeyer insisted. "You need to rest."

"I had to come, Uncle." Marie held her handkerchief up to her mouth. There was no hiding the bright red stains now. "It's important."

"What could be more important than your health?" Drosselmeyer asked. "Your recovery?"

"Uncle, I am not recovering." Marie looked up at her mentor. The usual spark in his eye was absent, the mystery in his weathered expression gone. Instead, his face was filled with an emotion she'd rarely seen him wear: grief. He knew as well as she did she was dying.

"Is there nothing to be done?" Drosselmeyer asked, his gravelly voice low.

Marie shook her head.

"How long?" Drosselmeyer asked.

"Not very," Marie said. "The children—" She glanced past Drosselmeyer at his ballroom. It was not decorated yet for the Christmas party, but it would be very soon. "I had so hoped to celebrate one more Christmas with them."

She shivered, and Drosselmeyer steadied her. His hand practically fit around her whole arm; she had grown so thin.

"Perhaps you still shall," Drosselmeyer said encouragingly. "There is always hope."

"No, Uncle." Marie reached into her pouch and withdrew a shiny golden key. It reflected the ballroom's lamplight, the unique cogs at the top sparkling.

"I need you to give this to Clara for me," she instructed. "For Christmas. I've given Charles gifts for Louise and Fritz already. But this gift—I need it to come from you. She's old enough now—older than I was when we first discovered the Realms.

And I see so much of myself in her. It will mean the most to her, will help her after . . . I'm gone. She's ready."

Drosselmeyer took the key hesitantly. "Are you sure?" he asked. "Wouldn't you prefer to go there with her? To guide her?"

Marie nodded, triggering a coughing fit. Drosselmeyer comforted her as she doubled over, staying by her side until the worst subsided.

Tears stung Marie's eyes. "I had wanted to, so badly. But I waited too long. I thought I would get better, but it's only grown worse. I don't want to take her there like this. The Realms should be magical. She should experience them as they were meant to be experienced—with joy. Not sorrow."

Drosselmeyer knelt before her. "If that is your wish, then it is what I shall do," he assured her. "Have you been to the Realms to tell them? Do the regents know?"

"That's what I've come to do." Marie stood, her will overpowering her weakness. "I must go now, before I can't any longer. I've put it off for so long—it's all my fault. I dreaded telling Sugar Plum. She will be heartbroken. I never meant to do this to her. To abandon her."

"You're not abandoning her, child," Drosselmeyer said. "She will understand."

Marie couldn't help the small, pale smile that crossed her lips. "Even with three children of my own, you still call me 'child.'"

Now the old man smiled, too. "'Clever child' then, if you prefer. Now come, I will help you."

They began the trek up the steps. But Marie's legs couldn't support her weight. She collapsed, falling in a heap upon the staircase. Violent coughs racked her fragile frame.

"This is not a good idea," Drosselmeyer said in concern. "We must get you home."

"No," Marie wheezed. "I must tell them."

"They will understand," Drosselmeyer repeated. "You should be home with your family now."

Marie looked up, her eyes like glass.

"Oh, Uncle."

Drosselmeyer supported Marie back out from the estate and into the brisk autumn air.

Neither one of them had seen—neither one of them could know—that two eyes had been watching them from high up on the grandfather clock. A tiny witness had seen everything, but had not heard the words that passed between them.

A small figurine with a tuft of pink hair and angry tears trickling like melted sugar down her porcelain white cheeks.

CHAPTER 21
CLARA

"We're coming!" Dew Drop cried. "Lower the drawbridge!"

Guards snapped to attention, immediately turning a large wheel to lower the drawbridge leading onto the palace grounds. Phillip and Clara raced across, followed by the troops Dew Drop had guided out from the desolation of the Fourth Realm. They had made it back—they were safe.

And they had the key!

"Clara?" Sugar Plum called, stepping out from the shadows where she'd been hiding. She couldn't let the other regents know she had been a part of this renegade mission.

"I have it!" Clara exclaimed proudly. "I have the key!"

She held up the shiny golden key her mother had made so long ago.

Sugar Plum's face broke into an enormous smile.

"You wonderful girl!" she cheered, spinning Clara around in delight. She drew Clara in for a warm embrace, and for just the briefest of moments, Clara almost imagined it was her mother hugging her, proud of her success. She didn't even notice Sugar Plum take the key from her grasp before the Sweets Regent said, "Now quickly, to the Engine Room!"

Sugar Plum, Phillip, and Clara whisked through the palace and down the secret staircase to the Engine Room, Dew Drop trailing behind in a flurry of sparks. Guards were waiting there for them, ready to open the Engine Room door. Sugar Plum swept past and leaped up to the control panel, the golden key in hand.

"Put it in!" Dew Drop exclaimed, buzzing back and forth.

Sugar Plum held the key up. It glinted in the lamplight. "Finally," she whispered. "The Realms will get what they need. What they have waited so long for."

In one swift motion, she inserted the key into the keyhole.

But when she went to turn it—it didn't work. It wouldn't even budge. Sugar Plum tried again. Nothing. It remained firmly in place. Sugar Plum's expression melted from elation to fury as she tried forcing the key either way to no avail.

"It won't turn!" she cried in anger. *"Argh!"*

She flung the key onto a pile with all the other rejected keys of the past.

But Clara wasn't ready to give up. "It has to be the right key," she insisted. "Why would Mother Ginger want it otherwise?"

Clara picked the tiny golden treasure up from the pile and examined it. Its handle was in the shape of an ornate bow. But what was this? The bow could turn, changing the shape of the key's teeth.

"Look!" she cried. "It's got moving teeth and a dial on the bow. I think it might—yes! Look, Sugar Plum, the key changes shape!"

Sugar Plum's face instantly transformed back into the picture of eager perfection.

"Come along, Clara. Quickly! Mother Ginger's army will be upon us."

Clara stepped up to the control panel and fit the key in. But this time, she twisted the bow until the teeth matched the keyhole inserts. With a satisfying *thunk,* it sank into place. Clara turned it, and it went smoothly to the right without any resistance.

Everyone watched. And waited.

For a nerve-racking moment, nothing happened. Then, very slowly, gears began to turn, screeching as though they hadn't been oiled in years. Pistons began to pump, steam hissed, and fan belts whirred. A deep chugging sound echoed from some-where deep inside the Engine.

Clara watched proudly as the Engine hummed to life. Her mother's finest invention, working once more.

Sugar Plum watched as well, her smile oddly twisted. Then she walked over to a bucket and picked it up. She carried it to the platform and dumped out its contents.

Toy tin soldiers—at least two dozen of them—scattered beneath the Engine's tube.

"Uh—I think it was designed to make one at a time," Clara pointed out.

"Oh, we haven't time for that, I'm afraid," Sugar Plum said smoothly. "Just press the button, my sweet."

"But—" Clara protested.

"The Realms are at stake, Clara, darling dearest." Sugar Plum's eyes flashed. "Press the button."

Uncertainly, Clara did as she was told. She stepped up to the control panel and pushed a large red button.

A bright beam of light shot out onto the platform, hitting all the tin soldiers at once. One by one, they each enlarged, spring-ing to life! But something was wrong. Instead of full-sized soldiers like Phillip or the guards, these toys were transforming into half-sized figures, deformed and with sinister faces.

"You see?" Clara said. "We shouldn't have put more than one—"

"I see exactly," Sugar Plum said, silencing her, her focus entirely upon the growing army of grotesque tin soldiers. "Attention!"

The army turned to face her, smiling and scowling.

"Quick march!" Sugar Plum ordered.

The tin soldiers marched off the platform, heading for the doorway that led up the staircase.

Clara watched in confusion as Sugar Plum took an even larger bucket of soldiers and dumped it onto the platform.

"Thank you so much, Clara," Sugar Plum said sweetly. "Guards, lock them up."

"What—?" Clara sputtered as the guards who had let them into the Engine Room grabbed hold of her by the arms.

"Take your hands off her!" Phillip demanded. He drew his sword, but a guard quickly knocked it from his grasp using the hilt of his weapon. He hit Phillip across the back, overpowering him. The guards pinned Phillip's and Clara's arms behind their backs and forced them toward the door. Meanwhile, Sugar Plum dumped bucket upon bucket of tin soldiers onto the platform.

"Sugar Plum, please—what are you doing?" Clara begged, twisting back to look at her mother's friend.

"Your mother was all for letting everybody decide things together, bless her," Sugar Plum sneered. All pretense of sweetness and decorum were gone from Sugar Plum's manner. Her voice dripped with disdain. "Leaving four regents to 'work together' while she was just far too busy with her sweet family to bother stopping by. I was her first creation—*me*. *I* was perfect. If anyone was meant to run the Realms, it was *me*. Not those bumbling idiots Shiver and Hawthorn. And certainly not Mother Ginger."

Clara watched in horror as Sugar Plum hit the Engine button again.

And the sickening, horrible truth dawned on her.

She lied. Clara's mind reeled while rows upon rows of twisted, ugly tin soldiers popped to life like hideous toy goblins. *It was all lies! Sugar Plum never wanted to save the Realms. She just wanted me to get her the key so she could make her own army. To rule them! Mother Ginger tried to warn me, but I didn't listen.*

"It was *you* who destroyed the Fourth Realm, wasn't it?"

Clara struggled angrily against the guards. "Mother Ginger isn't the traitor—you are!"

Sugar Plum walked over and gripped Clara's chin in her fingers.

"Clever girl," she mocked. "Isn't that what your mother used to call you? 'Clever girl'? Clearly not clever enough. What she saw in you is beyond me. But all her mistakes will now be rectified."

Sugar Plum plucked another bucket from the ground and hurled its contents onto the platform. She pressed the button.

"Take them away."

CHAPTER 22
SUGAR PLUM

"She's abandoned us!"

Sugar Plum paced furiously in Marie's bedchamber, clutching the queen's crown so tightly it cut into her palm.

Mother Ginger stood in the corner of the room. The old woman watched patiently as Sugar Plum vented her frustration. "Our queen has not abandoned anyone," she said in her typical stern manner. "If she is absent, it is because she has good reason."

"She never comes anymore!" Sugar Plum snapped. "She doesn't care."

"Sugar Plum, you have to understand that Marie is not like us," Mother Ginger said. "She's not a toy. She's human—and fragile. Her illness is grave. She's not well enough to visit as often as you'd like."

"She was well enough to visit the old man," Sugar Plum scoffed.

Ages had passed since Sugar Plum had witnessed Marie

and Drosselmeyer's conversation in the ballroom. Marie had seemed a little unwell, yes. She'd coughed and stumbled upon the staircase, but the old man had helped her up, so it couldn't have been that bad, could it? Sugar Plum hadn't been able to hear what the two discussed. She only knew one thing for certain: Marie had come—and left—without visiting them.

And now, it was as though she had vanished. No word, no warning. Just gone.

"She was *right here*!" Sugar Plum exclaimed. "And she *still* didn't come."

"Perhaps she was too ill to do so," Mother Ginger said.

"Then the old man should have carried her."

"That's absurd," Mother Ginger told her. "You're seeing what you want to see."

"I saw enough."

"What are you expecting, my dear?" Mother Ginger asked. "For Marie to remain in the Realms forever?"

"She has an obligation to us," Sugar Plum insisted. She waved Marie's crown. "She is our queen. She can't just create us and then cast us aside, like . . . like—"

"Toys?" Mother Ginger finished.

Sugar Plum's cheeks flushed pink. "Well, we are not toys now, are we?"

"You're right," Mother Ginger said. "We are not toys now. We are regents. And Marie has entrusted us with the safety of the Realms. She is treating us as leaders."

"So you're saying it doesn't matter to you?" Sugar Plum asked bitterly. "It doesn't bother you at all that our queen—our creator—has forgotten all about us?"

"You speak too harshly, Sugar Plum." Mother Ginger shook her head. "I do not believe Marie has forgotten us. But she has a family and children that she needs to take care of."

Now Sugar Plum's face grew dark. "*We* are her family. Not those dusty, dirty children. *I* was with her from the beginning. *I* am perfect."

"You may look perfect." Mother Ginger frowned. "But you are acting like a spoiled child."

"How dare you!" Sugar Plum stepped up in Mother Ginger's face. "You have no *idea* the lifetime of memories I share with Marie."

"You're right, I do not." Mother Ginger never wavered. "But I know what Marie wanted most for you was your happiness. For you to grow closer with the others in the Realms. To find your family in us."

If Sugar Plum hadn't been so furious, she would have laughed. "What, with you?" she mocked. "And Shiver, and Hawthorn? Bumbling fools. What sort of family is that?"

"The family Marie created for you," Mother Ginger replied.

Sugar Plum huffed and turned away. She looked down at the crown in her hands. "Fine. If Marie is too busy with her darling *family* to be queen, then I shall rule in her place."

"The citizens of the Realms won't have it," Mother Ginger warned. "We are supposed to work together. At Marie's command."

"But Marie—isn't—here!" Sugar Plum flung the crown upon the ground. Her shoulders shuddered with rage. She had never felt so angry, so desperate in her existence.

Why couldn't Marie just have come back?

Mother Ginger calmly stepped over and picked up the crown. "We must work together now," she repeated. "No one regent was ever meant to be queen."

Sugar Plum remained turned away so the old woman wouldn't see the bitter tears stinging her eyes.

"Then I will go *find* our queen," she hissed. "And bring her home."

CHAPTER 23

CLARA

The door to the palace observation tower slammed shut, leaving Clara and Phillip trapped inside. Phillip pounded on the door.

"She tricked us, Phillip," Clara said miserably. "She only wanted the key to take control. I thought she was my friend."

Phillip shook his head. "She fooled all of us."

Suddenly, a massive clamor outside in the courtyard drew their attention. Phillip and Clara raced to the observation room balcony. From their vantage point, they could see a legion of evil tin soldiers marching their way straight past the drawbridge guards and onto the bridge leading to the Fourth Realm.

"They're going to attack," Phillip realized.

"That's what Sugar Plum meant by 'rectifying' my mother's mistakes." Clara's eyes grew wide. "She's going to destroy Mother Ginger once and for all, and take control of all the Realms!"

Just then, the door to the observation room banged open.

Guards threw Shiver and Hawthorn unceremoniously to the floor before locking the door again.

"Shiver? Hawthorn?" Clara hurried to help the regents to their feet.

"Alas, you have been captured as well, my dear?" Shiver asked.

"I'm afraid it's all my fault," Clara answered with remorse. "I've let you down. I let my mother down."

"There's still time to stop Sugar Plum," Phillip insisted. "We need to get out of here."

He and Clara took another look out over the balcony, down the dizzying drop to the ground below. It was at least several hundred feet. Short of flying, there was no escape.

"It's hopeless." Clara sank to the floor.

How could I have been so blind? she thought woefully. How could she not have seen Sugar Plum's deception sooner? All she had wanted was to know her mother's final message. But perhaps in doing so, she had been too eager to retrieve the key without asking the right questions, as any inventor should. As her mother had taught her. Had her own selfish desire caused this tragedy? The thought filled Clara with guilt.

Clara buried her face in her hands.

Then, out of nowhere, her mother's favorite melody began playing.

Everyone looked around in confusion before realizing the muffled music was coming from Clara's dress. It was her mother's music box.

Clara gently removed the treasure from her pocket and opened it. The gold-framed mirrors glinted inside.

If only there had been a message from you, Mother, Clara thought sadly. *If only you could have told me what you wanted me to know.*

A ray of sunlight caught one of the mirrors, illuminating Clara's face. She studied her reflection, wishing she could see her mother in it.

But it was just her in the mirror. Clara. The same brown eyes looking back at her as they had her whole life—the ones her mother used to say sparkled with a clever mechanic's gleam.

Everything you need is inside.

And then she understood. A smile slowly spread across her face.

"Everything you need is inside."

Clara got to her feet, new determination welling up inside of her.

"I've got it!" she cried triumphantly. "Everything you need is inside!"

"But isn't it empty?" Phillip asked, confused.

"Not quite," Clara said. "It has the mirror. Don't you see, Phillip? She was talking about me!"

Clara realized her mother *had* left her a message after all. She'd wanted Clara to know that she believed in her. And now Clara had to believe in herself. All Clara's time spent tinkering, her days buried in tools and gears and metal bits—everything she'd learned from her mother, her lessons, her tricks, her tests—it had all culminated in this.

Her mother had invented the Engine.

Which meant Clara could figure out a way to stop it.

With a flurry of energy, she tore a piece of fabric off her dress and headed to a nearby telescope. Quickly, she unscrewed the lens. Then she turned to Phillip.

"I'll need your buttons, I'm afraid."

"My buttons?" Phillip asked. "Clara, what are you doing?"

"Assembling a tool kit," Clara explained. "I know how to stop her. Get me to the Engine Room and I can stop Sugar Plum."

Hawthorn shook his head. "That's a lovely sentiment, my dear, but—"

"Your belt, please, Hawthorn." Clara held out her hand expectantly. "And that pin, Shiver."

The regents shared a look of uncertainty, but complied. Clara placed the makeshift tools in her improvised fabric pouch and wrapped it shut.

"But how are we going to get you out of here?" Phillip asked.

"There's a way," Clara said, resolute. "There's always a way."

She looked around the observation room. There were telescopes and compasses. Charts and astrolabes.

And hanging high above them all, a heavy gilded chandelier, dangling from a long rope.

"That's it," Clara breathed.

She had an idea.

A short while later, the chandelier lay on the ground, the rope coiled up at their feet. Phillip had secured the end of the rope to the middle strut of the balcony while Clara unscrewed a heavy candelabra. She handed it to Phillip. Her plan was ready.

"Shall I?" Phillip asked.

Clara shook her head. "Ladies first."

"I'll be right behind you," Phillip promised.

Clara tied the other end of the rope to her waist. Then she took a deep breath and swung her legs over the balcony railing.

Carefully, she began climbing down the side of the tower, gripping the rope tightly. She tried not to look down, lest her palms grow too sweaty from nerves.

Slowly but surely, she made her way to her destination: a banner pole that stuck out from the side of the tower. She steadied herself upon it and cautiously inched out. Once she had reached the end, she balanced precariously and looked back up to Phillip. He was holding the long slack of rope. He quickly untied the other end from the balcony rail and attached it to the heavy piece of chandelier as a counterweight.

"Further back," she instructed Phillip. "Further."

"What the devil?! Clara!" Hawthorn cried from inside the observation room.

Shiver shared his horror. "My dear, that looks most insecure!"

"Insecure? *Insecure?*" Hawthorn exclaimed. "Come back off there, my girl!"

But Clara only had eyes for Phillip.

"Stop there," she ordered. "Are you ready?"

"Ready." Phillip nodded nervously. "Are you sure about this?"

"It's just the laws of physics," Clara said.

"And they always work, these laws?" Phillip asked.

Clara glanced down at the courtyard, so very far below.

She gulped. "Always . . . as far as I know." Then she shook away her fear. "On my mark?"

Phillip nodded. He held the counterweight at the ready.

"Three—"

Clara took a deep breath.

"Two—"

She thought of her mother.

"One."

She dropped.

CHAPTER 24

SUGAR PLUM

P ine needles scraped Sugar Plum's flawless skin as she crashed through the forest. It was dark—far too dark for the Sweets Regent to be racing through the Fourth Realm. She might stumble upon a root, or worse, crash into the remains of an afternoon tea party and muss her perfect dress, wreck her perfectly coifed hair, or scar her perfect face.

But Sugar Plum was on a mission. And for once, perfection would not help her accomplish it.

Overhead, bands of deep purple clouds streaked the nighttime sky. An enormous Ferris wheel loomed over the trees, imposing, like a monster. The citizens of the Land of Amusement had long since retired to the city center, leaving their remnants of games and revelry strewn about like debris in the night. *Why did Marie even create this realm?* Sugar Plum thought with disgust. *Even the carousel animals look grotesque.*

She pressed on, the forest growing denser and denser until,

finally, she reached it: the place only Marie and Sugar Plum knew of. The entrance to the other world.

To the untrained eye, it seemed nothing more than an old, uprooted pine tree, decayed and forgotten. But beyond its gnarled roots, deep within the hollow tunnel, lay the passage to the real world through which Marie came.

Sugar Plum grasped the rough edge of a dry root and peered as far as she could down the tunnel. It was useless—all she could see was velvety blackness. The passageway's secret could only be unveiled by stepping through into the unknown.

Things that exist in the Realms can't exist in the real world. Marie's words haunted Sugar Plum as she weighed her choice.

Her heart pounding, Sugar Plum stepped inside.

She waited, but nothing happened. She was all right—so far.

You can't come with me. The warning echoed as she took another step forward. And then another. *I think you would go back to being a doll.*

But Sugar Plum pushed on, running her silky hand against the wall of the hollow tree to keep her steady. She didn't feel any different. *Perhaps Marie was wrong,* she thought. Perhaps she *could* cross over into the real world. She was special, after all. The first toy Marie had brought to life. Surely that meant something?

Then, with a start, she realized the rough wall had grown smooth, like polished wood. She was at the other side.

Things that exist in the Realms can't exist in the real world.

"Maybe I'm special," she whispered to herself.

The faint outline of a doorway slid into view.

You can't come with me.

"Maybe I can."

She stretched out her hand. It brushed a cold doorknob.

I think you would go back to being a doll.

"How can you know?"

Sugar Plum turned the knob and opened the door.

Yellow light washed into the corridor. Sugar Plum shielded her eyes.

She didn't quite understand what she was seeing. It looked like the door opened into a hallway. But . . . it was a very unsettling hallway. Not at all like the crystal-chandelier-lined corridors of the palace, with their colorful topiaries and ice sculptures. This hall was dim and dusty, with red-and-gold checkered flooring and wallpaper stamped with rows of mouse silhouettes. Gas lamps flickered, their dreary light illuminating even drearier imperfection.

Sugar Plum examined it all, staying very, very still. One

more step, and she would be in the real world. This ugly place didn't look like anything special, though. It didn't look like a place she even wanted to be a part of. But Marie had left her no choice, had she? She had abandoned them. And now Sugar Plum had to risk everything to bring their queen home.

She reached a hesitant hand just over the tip of the threshold.

What was that? she thought, withdrawing again. Had her hand sparkled? For just a moment, it seemed like magic had floated off her skin.

But perhaps she had imagined it?

She went to move her hand over the threshold again.

I think you would go back to being a doll.

She snapped her hand back, as though burned.

What if Marie had been right? What if she *did* go back to being a doll as soon as she crossed the doorway? Was Sugar Plum just supposed to give up her throne—her entire existence—because Marie hadn't felt like bothering with them anymore?

She shook her head. *This is nonsense,* she thought. *Clearly I am unique. Clearly I have power. If I want it badly enough, I can make it happen. I am imagination brought to life.*

She took a step back, breathed heavily, and started to leap forward across the threshold.

But before she'd even passed by a hairbreadth, she threw out her arms, hitting the doorframe and preventing herself from crossing the full distance.

This isn't fair! She clenched her teeth. *Why should I have to risk everything to bring Marie home? It should be Hawthorn, or Shiver, or that horrible Mother Ginger. Anyone but me!*

She stared angrily at the hideous checkered floor. Bitter tears stained her cheeks.

I'm sure Mother Ginger would love *that.* Her thoughts turned dark. *That vile old woman would just love for me to never come back. For me to vanish, the way Marie did. Then she and Hawthorn and Shiver and the rest of the sniveling lot could "work together" in wretched complacency because no one—no one!—knows how to rule the Realms as well as I do. If anyone should be destroyed, it's Mother Ginger, not me!*

She glared forward, consumed by rage. And that's when she saw it. One of the mice on the patterned wallpaper moved! She screamed and recoiled in disgust.

But what was this? The beady-eyed little rodent scurried along, yet the wallpaper pattern remained intact. Had it actually come from the wall? Had it been there the whole time?

"The real world is repulsive," Sugar Plum muttered.

Then . . . the mouse started moving toward her. Sugar Plum backed farther into the dark corridor. Yet the mouse continued—beyond the threshold, and straight for Sugar Plum's feet!

It gained speed, creeping right up to her sugar-coated shoe.

Sugar Plum shrieked. "Get away, you filthy rodent!" She kicked at the vermin. Her blow knocked the mouse back, dazing it, but only for a moment. It regained its bearings and started coming back toward her. To her horror, more mice were joining behind it. She had no idea where they'd come from—wallpaper or holes or some other filthy corner of the real world. But they were all intently sniffing out the sugar in her clothing. They were drawn by sweets.

"Loathsome vermin," Sugar Plum snarled, ready to slam the door in their path. "It's no wonder we don't have vulgar creatures like you in the Realms. You would eat it all, destroy it with your nasty teeth and—"

Suddenly, she stopped. She watched the mice piling up at the doorway, eager for a taste of the sweet, sweet candy only a realm like the Land of Sweets could provide.

"Yes, you would destroy it, wouldn't you, my sweets," she said quietly.

If she hadn't known better, she would have sworn the mice were listening.

An idea slowly dawned on her. A terrible, horrible idea. Of justice. Of vengeance. Of something she'd never before thought of doing, but really, what choice did she have? What choice had Marie left her?

Sugar Plum leaned in closer to the clamoring, scratching mice.

"Let me tell you a little story, my pets," she whispered. "Of a land where you can have sweets to your hearts' content, as long as you do as I say."

"It can't be." Hawthorn paced back and forth nervously in the throne room.

"Are you absolutely sure?" Shiver asked, tapping his fingertips together.

"I'm afraid so." Sugar Plum's expression was the picture of perfect concern as she met secretly with Shiver and Hawthorn late the next evening. "I heard it with my own ears. Mother Ginger never meant for another soul to catch her. But her words were crystal clear: 'I shall rule the Realms.'"

"And she said this in our dear Queen Marie's very own bed-chambers?" Hawthorn asked, aghast.

Sugar Plum nodded. *"While* wearing her crown."

Shiver scoffed. "It's unthinkable. For one regent to plot sub-version of the others is simply . . . simply . . ."

"Evil?" Sugar Plum suggested helpfully.

"Exactly!" Shiver exclaimed.

"Then, my dear regents, perhaps you should sit down for what I am about to tell you." Sugar Plum guided the two men to their thrones. "For while I was in the Fourth Realm the other day, I saw something truly horrific."

"What? What did you see?" Hawthorn asked, his voice a raspy whisper.

"I went to speak with Mother Ginger," Sugar Plum explained. "To see if I could dissuade her from her dark venture before bring-ing it to your esteemed attention. But sadly, I never made it to her, because as I passed through the forest, I encountered a—a—"

She covered her petal-pink lips and turned away.

"A what, my dear?" Shiver pressed.

Sugar Plum turned to face them. "A mouse."

"A mouse!" the two regents cried in alarm.

"Surely Mother Ginger is not so reckless," Hawthorn fretted.

"Such a creature could destroy our very world." Shiver passed a shaking hand across his face.

"Marie did tell me stories of the wild animals in the real world," Sugar Plum conceded. "I wouldn't have even known it was a mouse but for Marie's stern guidance that should such a creature ever be spotted here, we should warn her immediately."

"She gave us the same warning," Hawthorn concurred.

"She warned us all!" Shiver exclaimed.

"But now, we have no queen *to* warn." Hawthorn slumped into his throne.

"And without her, I fear the safety of the Realms is at risk," Shiver concluded.

Sugar Plum turned to the beautiful case at the center of the throne room where Marie's old crown had been placed delicately on display.

"Not necessarily," she said to them.

"What do you mean?" Shiver asked.

"Yes, what do you have in mind?" Hawthorn added.

Neither regent saw the fleeting smile that passed across Sugar Plum's lips.

"Has either of you dear men ever heard of . . . a drawbridge?"

CHAPTER 25

SUGAR PLUM

"Mice!" people screamed as they came running across the bridge, away from the Fourth Realm. "Mice are coming! They're destroying everything!"

Chaos echoed behind the fleeing citizens as legions of furry rodents overran the Land of Amusement, devouring tea party delicacies and swarming over carnival rides and buildings alike. Everyone streamed across the bridge in a panic, desperate to escape the onslaught.

"What's happening?" Mother Ginger cried in alarm, the only one staying behind in the Fourth Realm. "How can this be? *How* did this happen?"

She looked on in horror as waves of mice flooded past . . . *eating* everything in sight! Her entire realm was being devoured, crumbling before her very eyes.

Meanwhile, some distance away, Sugar Plum stood atop the palace's observation tower balcony. From her vantage point, she watched the devastation through a telescope. Dew Drop sat on her shoulder, nibbling on a miniature bag of popcorn.

They saw the old woman cry in dismay as her prized Ferris wheel came toppling down, crashing into the trees with a thunderous groan.

Sugar Plum smiled. "Well done," she whispered to Dew Drop.

"It's a show, I'll tell you that!" Dew Drop agreed.

Of course, what no one realized was that just hours before, Dew Drop had completed a special mission on Sugar Plum's behalf: the tiny fairy had sprinkled Sugar Starter powder around the base of every building, every ride, and every carnival game in the Land of Amusement. Ingenious stuff, really. One of Marie's finer imaginative creations, if Sugar Plum did say so herself. When Marie had first invented it, she had blathered on and on about chemistry and compounds and a whole bunch more "real world" nonsense Sugar Plum hadn't really paid attention to. But what Sugar Plum did know was that bakers in the Land of Sweets regularly used the powder to turn anything instantly into crystallized sugar, from glass lamps and vases to even ribbons and roses. When used properly, the results were lovely. However, if used improperly—say, on the foundation blocks of an entire city—and then exposed to the gobbling mouths of sugar-loving vermin . . . well, the results could be devastating.

But, of course, why would anyone ever think of something so dreadful?

Through her telescope, Sugar Plum saw Mother Ginger wail in heartbreak as her beautiful realm came crumbling down to the ground, plumes of sugar dust and debris soaring into the air while the unmistakable shrieks of mice echoed far enough for even those in the palace courtyard to hear.

Then the old woman turned. It was as though she were staring directly at Sugar Plum.

Sugar Plum tilted her head to address Dew Drop. "Tell them to raise the drawbridge."

"Aye, aye, Pinky." Dew Drop whizzed off in a trail of sparks.

Leisurely, Sugar Plum made her way down from the tower. She walked down the palace steps, across the courtyard, and up to the new watchtowers cleverly placed on either side of the drawbridge.

Shiver and Hawthorn were waiting for her there. Together,

they witnessed the inaugural raising of the drawbridge just as Mother Ginger came running out of the smoke and ruin of the Fourth Realm, the only citizen to not escape.

"What *is* this?!" Mother Ginger cried in rage. She skidded to a stop at the edge of the bridge. Rushing water thundered far below in the chasm. "What have you done?"

"It is your own undoing," Sugar Plum announced solemnly. "The consequence of your evil plot."

"*My* plot?" Mother Ginger exclaimed.

"Sugar Plum is right," Shiver called. "We could not allow you to bring mice into the Realms."

"Just look what they've done to your own land!" Hawthorn cried. "Those vile creatures have destroyed everything! They would have done the same to our realms, too."

Shiver shook his head gravely. "No one regent was ever meant to be queen."

"No one regent—" Mother Ginger spluttered. She glared at Sugar Plum, her eyes burning with fury. "This is all *your* doing! You have filled their heads with lies! *You* let the mice in and have destroyed my realm all because of your childish impertinence!"

Sugar Plum sighed. "I wish I could forgive you, Mother

Ginger," she said. "But your obsession with power has blinded you—driven you mad. And now your realm has paid the price."

"Don't you realize she has fooled you?" Mother Ginger pleaded with Shiver and Hawthorn. "She must have lured the mice in with the promise of sweets, the way only a Sweets Regent could. *Sugar Plum* is the one behind this. She has been desperate ever since Marie left. She wanted to rule the Realms in Marie's place—as vengeance!"

For the briefest of moments, Shiver and Hawthorn seemed to consider the possibility. Doubt crossed their faces.

"She attempts to deceive us," Sugar Plum whispered to them. "To separate us with mistrust. Do not let her fool you."

Sugar Plum fixed her gaze upon Hawthorn. "Or the mice shall surely trample and choke your flowers."

Then she looked to Shiver. "And crack your ice glacier, sending your realm into the abyss."

A perfect tear trickled down her delicate cheek. "And they will devour my beautiful Land of Sweets, until all that Marie created for us is no more. Fallen to ashes."

She held their hands. "We cannot let her divide us."

Shiver and Hawthorn regained their confidence. They turned to Mother Ginger.

"Mother Ginger, you are hereby banished," Shiver proclaimed. "You will remain in the Fourth Realm, its destruction a constant reminder of the consequences of your selfish ambition."

"And those nasty rodents shall never set foot—I mean paw—in our realms, as long as we have anything to say about it!" Hawthorn shouted.

As they spoke, Mother Ginger's eyes never left Sugar Plum's face.

Just for the old woman, Sugar Plum flashed a smile. In the blink of an eye it was gone, as though it had never even appeared.

"We wish it didn't have to be this way," Sugar Plum told her. "If only you could have been content to work with us, together, as Marie desired."

CHAPTER 26

CLARA

Clara plummeted toward the courtyard at dizzying speed.

Shiver and Hawthorn covered their eyes. Surely, she was done for.

"Come on," Phillip whispered urgently under his breath.

The counterweight whipped around the banner pole—once, twice, three times, spinning faster and faster as the rope grew shorter and shorter. The coils began to slide around the banner pole, the rope straining between the opposing weights of Clara and the heavy chandelier piece. And then, just as Clara predicted, it happened: the laws of physics became apparent. The friction of the rope slowed Clara's descent. She dropped a hundred feet, then fifty, then twenty, all the while losing speed until, finally, she stopped, her feet just touching the ground. The entire ordeal lasted only a matter of seconds. But for Clara and the others, it was enough excitement for a lifetime.

"It worked!" Shiver and Hawthorn bounced up and down, hugging one another.

Phillip breathed a sigh of relief. "Clever indeed," he whispered.

Clara untied the rope from her waist and waved to Phillip. Now it was his turn.

He quickly took hold of the rope and began rappelling down the side of the tower.

Clara watched, impressed.

"Did you learn that in soldier training?" she quipped when he reached the ground beside her.

Phillip winked. "We can't all take the easy way down. Come! We must hurry."

The friends stealthily made their way through the palace grounds, keeping out of sight and searching for a way to get in. But all the entrances to the castle were securely guarded by Sugar Plum's evil tin soldiers.

"There's no way in," Clara whispered.

Suddenly, a squeak caught their attention.

A mouse was perched on a ledge just behind Phillip's shoulder! Phillip recoiled.

"Back away!" he warned Clara. "Mice!"

"Wait—I think it's okay." Clara looked more closely at the furry creature. It wasn't just any mouse—it was the one she had first encountered when she'd entered the Realms. The one with an angry scar running across its eye.

"It's Mouserinks!" Clara exclaimed.

Taking a chance, she held out her hand. Mouserinks sniffed it, and his features softened. He scurried into her palm, and she gently stroked down his fur. Just like that, he looked like a cute little mouse.

"I think he's here to help," Clara whispered to Phillip. "Aren't you, Mouserinks?"

The tiny mouse gave another squeak and hopped down from her hand. He ran over to an ornate hatch cover in the middle of the cobblestoned road.

"He knows a way in," Phillip said, realization dawning.

Clara grinned. "Mice always do."

The hatch led Clara and Phillip down a long ladder deep into a shaft, which seemed to have no bottom. They climbed down and down, finally reaching a long tunnel. The sound of rushing water echoed from its depths. Mouserinks scurried ahead and out of sight.

"This way," Clara said, leading Phillip onward.

Together, they trekked down the shadowy corridor before coming upon an old, rusting gate. They opened it . . . and were met by a heart-stopping sight: a perilous rocky ledge overlooking the raging river that surrounded the palace. Clara and Phillip peered down—and gulped. The drop was treacherous, the rock wall slick and crumbling. Not far away, a waterfall thundered, spinning the massive wheels that powered the palace.

And the Engine Room, Clara realized.

That must be what Mouserinks wanted them to find. If she could get to the waterwheels, that was her way in. It had to be.

Meanwhile, far above them, the bridge leading to the Fourth Realm was in sight. Phillip and Clara watched Sugar Plum's tin soldiers marching across, battling Mother Ginger's mice and Polichinelles. The soldiers were strong, and there were too many—they were winning. If Clara and Phillip didn't hurry, there wouldn't be a Fourth Realm to save.

"You have to go back," Clara urged Phillip. "You have to stop Sugar Plum's army."

"How?" Phillip asked.

"Find a way, Phillip," Clara insisted. "You can do it. I believe in you."

Gratitude mingled with worry crossed Phillip's face as Clara stepped out onto the treacherous rock ledge.

"What about you?" he asked in concern.

"I've got what I need." Clara gripped the rock wall, steadfast. "This is for me. Go!"

Phillip gave her a last look. "Good luck," he said.

Then he was gone, racing back down the tunnel. And Clara was on her own.

She looked to her destination and continued along the perilous crags. Several times her feet slipped, but she managed to hang on, her hands sorely scraped from the jagged stone. Farther and farther she climbed, her arms and shoulders aching with the strain. Suddenly, she felt a cracking beneath her feet. She jumped ahead, clinging tightly to the wall as a large chunk of ledge broke away from where she had just been standing. There was no ledge any longer—and no going back.

Very slowly, she inched her way closer to the pounding waterwheel. Good hand- and footholds were becoming harder to find. She dug her fingernails in, the rocks slick with water spray.

Holding tightly with one hand, she felt around with the other, trying to locate a secure grip. Her hand slid into a deep crack—

And a flock of birds flew out!

Startled, she yelled, her voice lost against the roaring water. Her grip slipped, and she swung outward by her remaining hand, feet dangling free over the roaring chasm below!

The birds flew upward, and Clara swung back into balance, miraculously finding the handhold again. She hugged the rock wall, breathing hard.

"Everything you need is inside," she repeated to herself, over and over. "Everything you need is inside."

The paddles of the waterwheel were in front of her now. Curtains of water poured down. Shakily, she looked up to scan the wheel's encasement. There had to be an entrance into the palace's Engine Room somewhere. There *had* to be. . . .

"There!" Clara cried. At the pinnacle of the waterwheel was an opening. That was it! The way into the Engine Room!

Only there was no rock wall to climb to reach it. The only way up was—

Clara watched the fast-moving waterwheel paddles fly past.

"You've got to be kidding me," she murmured.

Her heart raced. But she stayed strong.

"I can do this," she said.

The paddles whipped past. One wrong move—any wrong move—and she'd be sent spiraling to the bottom of the chasm.

"On three," she whispered to herself. "One—two—three!"

She lurched forward, just barely grabbing the lip of the whizzing paddle. It soared upward, carrying her along with it. Her hair whipped back—her stomach churned—and then, somehow, miraculously . . .

Thump!

Clara flew through the opening into the Engine Room, landing on the cold stone floor. She lay there for a long moment, bedraggled, breathless, exhausted.

But she had made it.

She swallowed hard and sat up. Every muscle in her body screamed in protest.

But she ignored the pain.

"Time to get to work," she said.

Precious moments ticked away. Clara worked furiously on the Engine's control panel. Her tools were spread out on the floor, having helped her complete the first part of her plan. She'd run a long length of wire around the room, close to the ground. It connected to a pin, which held the rope of the Engine Room's heavy chandelier.

That had been the easy bit. Now was the hard part: reimagining the operation of the Engine itself.

Clara nimbly sorted through the tangle of wires, trying to make sense of her mother's handiwork.

"How do I change it, Mother?" she whispered under her breath. "How do I reverse the mechanism?"

She followed one of the thin wires back to where it connected to a magnetic block, just like the magnet that had powered Drosselmeyer's mechanical model of swans upon a lake, but on a much, much larger scale.

"Aha," she whispered.

She took Shiver's pin, which had been clamped between her teeth, and used it to unfasten the screw that attached the wire to the block. She found the opposite wire, and studied them in her fingertips.

"I hope this works," she whispered to herself.

Suddenly, a massive noise rattled her. But it hadn't come from inside the palace—it had come from outside the opening through which she'd entered, out on the water. It sounded as though something huge had collapsed!

She ran to the crevice leading to the wheel and peered out through the rushing curtains of water. She gasped. Through the spray, she witnessed the bridge to the Fourth Realm collapsing, Sugar Plum's tin soldier army falling along with it!

"Phillip's done it!" Clara realized with a thrill of pride. "He's stopped the army!"

She clapped her hands in delight. But then, a terrible thought struck her.

"Which means Sugar Plum will be coming to make more soldiers." Her heart pounded. "I don't have much time."

She bolted back to the control panel and tinkered feverishly. One wire here—another there. Crisscrossed and redirected and screwed back into place. She had just secured the final bit when . . .

Clang!

The door to the Engine Room burst open.

And a figure loomed in the doorway.

 CHAPTER 27

CLARA

"Y ou!" Sugar Plum shouted furiously.

The Sweets Regent strode into the room, Dew Drop trailing close behind. The fairy's sparks were not so pretty now—they were flaming red.

"Did you really think you could stop me?" Sugar Plum advanced upon Clara. "When an entirely new army is always at my fingertips?"

She was about to strike when, suddenly, she tripped the wire Clara had run about the room. It pulled the pin holding the chandelier from the wall, and the entire fixture came crashing down. Clara jumped back just in time. The chandelier landed around Sugar Plum, trapping her like a heavy golden cage.

For a moment, Sugar Plum seemed startled. Then her face flooded with rage.

"Foolish child!" she shrieked.

"I believed you," Clara shouted back. "We all did. And you betrayed us!"

Sugar Plum clutched the chandelier cage bars. "Do you honestly think you can beat me? Your mother's most beautiful creation? The one who listened to her, understood her, and loved her most? Even as she abandoned us in favor of her *children*?"

"If you had really loved my mother, you wouldn't have destroyed so much of her creation," Clara retaliated. "But that's all at an end now, Sugar Plum."

Unexpectedly, Sugar Plum smiled, sickeningly sweet.

"Did you hear that, Dew Drop?" she sneered. "The little Stahlbaum girl says that's all at an end."

"Oh, boo-hoo," Dew Drop mocked, flitting around the cage.

"When actually"—Sugar Plum's eyes flashed—"it is just the beginning."

Without warning, she unfurled two massive, shimmering fairy wings. Clara gasped, stumbling back. Sugar Plum flapped her wings, beautiful and terrifying, lifting up off the ground . . . and straight out of the chandelier cage!

In that instant, Clara realized how much danger she was in. She darted sideways and rolled under the Engine's machinery. Meanwhile, Sugar Plum plucked up a handful of buckets and flew to the Engine's control panel. She twisted the key and then landed on the platform, dumping at least a hundred toy soldiers at her feet.

"Yes, hide, my sweet," Sugar Plum goaded. "That won't save you now. What a disappointment you must have been, little Clara. You with your awkward ways, tripping over your own feet, always some screwdriver in your hand, oil in your hair—goodness! How I watched you from the clock. *You?* Compared to *me*?"

Sugar Plum cackled.

"What *was* Marie thinking?"

Clara crept out from her hiding place, never taking her eyes off the Sweets Regent.

"She was proud of me for the person I am," Clara said, believing every word with her whole heart. "She loved me for that." She inched toward the control panel. "Every part of me." Another step. "And that was the very last thing she told me."

One step more. Clara was nearly there. Sugar Plum was right where she needed to be.

"You were right, Sugar Plum," Clara said. "I am every inch my mother's daughter."

In a flash, she bolted the final length to the control panel and slammed down the power button.

"Look out!" Dew Drop cried, whizzing up to Sugar Plum's shoulder.

But it was too late. Sugar Plum caught sight of her own reflection in the mirror Clara had carefully angled in front of the Engine's tube just before the laser beam flashed.

Clara shielded her eyes. The beam bounced off the mirror and zapped toward Sugar Plum and Dew Drop—a direct hit. They were enveloped in a brilliant burst of light.

And then, Clara heard the sound of something hitting the ground.

She slowly peeked out.

Sugar Plum and Dew Drop were gone.

Upon the platform rested a tiny hair clip in the shape of a fairy.

And a pretty porcelain doll.

CHAPTER 28

CLARA

"Are you sure we can't convince you to stay?"

Phillip and Clara stood high on the palace balcony, watching citizens celebrate in the courtyard below. Ballerinas danced, showering flower petals upon the cobblestoned paths while children laughed and tried to catch them. Bakers passed out victory treats; fairies dressed as snow angels blew shimmering dust into the air like confetti; and in the garden, even the mice made merry, with miniature party tables set with sweets and pastries just for them.

"It won't be the same without you," Phillip continued. A ray of sunlight caught the crown upon his head. He had been newly instated as the Regent of the Land of Sweets.

"I wish I could," Clara replied, now proudly wearing her mother's royal ball gown. Mouserinks sat upon her shoulder. "It's all so magical," Clara mused.

"Your mother's creation," Phillip pointed out. "And yours,

too, if you want. The Fourth Realm could use your inspiration. A tinkerer's touch."

Clara gazed out over the chasm to the Fourth Realm. Guards were already at work restoring the bridge. But this time, they were constructing it as one solid piece—no drawbridge. There was much work to be done in the Land of Amusement. Homes to rebuild, rides and games and a city to be brought back to life. But for the moment, the fog at least had lifted, and new buds were forming on the forest trees. It might take a while, but laughter would return to the Fourth Realm once more.

Behind Clara and Phillip, Shiver and Hawthorn presented Mother Ginger with her crown. The old woman was dressed in her regent finery again, her curly red hair coiled up into two regal poufs.

"Did Mother Ginger ever tell you *why* she made that horrible marionette?" Phillip whispered to Clara. "And . . . those *clowns*?"

Clara shook her head. "Not really. Something about needing to protect herself from the mice, and then Sugar Plum. She said that over time the mice realized Sugar Plum had tricked them and became loyal to her instead . . . but she didn't seem to want to talk about it too much."

Mother Ginger must have caught a hint of their discussion,

because she turned to Clara and nodded. Not exactly a smile, but more a look of wise approval.

"I think she wants to move past that," Clara told Phillip. "To forget the darkness and enjoy the light."

"As do we all," Phillip agreed.

Just then, Shiver, Hawthorn, and Mother Ginger all approached. Shiver was holding Marie's crown.

"Clara, the Regents of the Four Realms would be very honored if you would be our queen," Shiver announced.

Clara took the crown gingerly and admired it.

"This is what my mother wore?" she asked.

"Of course," Shiver replied.

Clara gazed at the crown for a long moment. It was lovely and ornate, its delicate silver scrollwork crafted expertly by hand, the way only a tinkerer could do.

The idea of being a queen was tempting . . . but . . .

"I'm afraid I can't," Clara said. "Though I love it here so much, and I love you all, I have to go back to where I came from. I'm so sorry."

She handed the crown back to Shiver.

"You see, there's somebody at home who needs me more than you do."

"But what will we do without a queen?" Shiver asked.

"It's quite the coronation conundrum," Hawthorn added.

But Clara just smiled. "My mother made every part of the Realms, and every part of you," she told them. "She lives in your memories and in your hearts. So, you see, in a strange way, you aren't really without a queen at all."

At that, the regents brightened.

Clara turned to gaze out toward the horizon. She could almost feel her mother's presence surrounding them. And filled with that warmth, she no longer felt lost or confused. Though the ache of missing her mother would never go away, she'd finally learned the full meaning of the music box's message: Marie had wanted, more than anything, for her family to be happy. She had given them all the gifts they needed to be whole, and Clara now understood that her mother's joy and laughter, ingenuity and grace, kindness and comfort and love all lived on through them. Through her. Everything she needed truly was inside.

"And in a strange way, I'm not really without a mother," Clara finished.

Shiver took Clara's hands. Phillip touched her shoulder.

"Farewell, then, Clara Stahlbaum," Shiver said. "Daughter of the Realms."

A little while later, Phillip stood with Clara at the base of the huge, uprooted tree in the Fourth Realm—the passage back to the real world. Clara was wearing her Christmas party dress again, her hair pinned, a bit haphazardly, to emulate the way Louise had done it.

The friends peered down the long, dark passageway.

"Will you come back to the Realms one day?" Phillip asked Clara.

"Of course I will," she said in reply. An idea suddenly came to her. "And maybe you could come to my world one day, too!"

"Is that possible?" Phillip asked.

Clara shrugged. "I think anything is possible, with just a bit of imagination. Perhaps we could work on an invention to make it possible, together."

"I'd like that," Phillip agreed.

"You could meet Fritz and Louise and my father!" Clara exclaimed.

Phillip tilted his head. "Are they like you?"

"Umm, they're a bit different," Clara admitted.

"I suppose they would be." Phillip grasped Clara's hand. "I've never met anybody like you, anywhere."

"Is that a good thing?" Clara asked.

"It's a wonderful thing," Phillip answered. "I'm going to miss you so much."

"I'll miss you, too." Clara hugged him tightly. "But when you miss me, you'll remember me. And that memory will make you smile."

"Really?" Phillip whispered.

"Really," Clara whispered back. "Goodbye, Phillip. Keep the Realms safe."

"I will," he promised. "Goodbye, Clara."

And with that, Clara stepped into the passageway, walking farther and farther, until she disappeared from sight.

CHAPTER 29
MARIE

Pine cones. Cinnamon. Roasted chestnuts and crackling firewood. The scents all mingled through Clara's bedroom window, cracked open just the tiniest bit to allow the fragrance of Christmastime spirit to float through. Marie breathed in deeply, and then closed the window.

"Tell me the story again!" Tiny Clara bounded onto her bed. The toddler's eyes sparkled, far from sleepy.

"Father Christmas will be here soon," Marie urged quietly. "You must hurry to sleep."

"Please tell me the story one more time." Clara pulled her blanket right up to her chin. "I promise to go to sleep after that."

"All right, my dear." Marie snuggled in next to her. "Once upon a time, there was a land. A very beautiful land, made entirely—"

"From imagination!" Clara had memorized the story and knew it by heart.

Marie nodded. "That's right. From imagination. Things were possible there that weren't possible anywhere else, you see. And each section had a purpose. There was a Land of Flowers, for beauty. A Land of Snowflakes, for memory. A Land of Sweets, for happiness. And a Land of Amusement."

"What was that one for?" Clara asked, already knowing the answer.

"That land, my darling, was for love." Marie stroked Clara's hair, enjoying the warmth of her precious daughter's tiny head against her chest.

"And the people of the land were all very special," Marie continued. "For they were, in fact, not people at all, but toys brought to life. They danced and played every day, the way only toys could do. And a beautiful fairy queen watched over them all, as lovely as a porcelain doll."

Clara's eyelids were beginning to droop now. She yawned.

"Is there really such a place, Mother?" she asked.

"There certainly could be," Marie whispered. "Anything is possible with just a bit of imagination."

"Have you been there?" Clara asked sleepily.

Marie smiled. "When I was little, I would sometimes feel scared or alone. But then I would dream of going to my own special world, where everything was lovely and perfect. And each time, I would imagine one new thing for my world—a new flower or game or even friend. And as long as I was there, I felt safe."

Clara's head grew heavy against Marie's shoulder. Her daughter was nodding off.

"And now it is time for you to have sweet dreams, too, my darling."

Marie gently shifted away, and Clara nestled into her pillow. Her eyes were already closed.

"Can I go there, too?" Clara asked, half in dream. "One day?"

Marie kissed Clara on the forehead, in awe of how much love and pride one tiny little person could bring. Her own clever little girl.

"I would like that very much."

CHAPTER 30

CLARA

Clara made her way through the dark passage to the distant, silhouetted doorway. Her hand brushed the cool doorknob, and she turned it. Just like that, she was back in Drosselmeyer's estate, the floor and wallpaper and gas lamps just the same as before.

But Clara was not the same.

She had been on an adventure. A grand adventure, made possible by her mother's imagination. And love.

Clara picked up her skirts and hurried down the hallway, through the double doors, and down the staircase sweeping into the great hall.

The Christmas party was still in full swing. Party guests danced and laughed. Children played with their gifts. It was as though Clara had been gone only a few minutes.

Drosselmeyer stood at the bottom of the staircase, gazing up at the grandfather clock. He turned as Clara approached.

"Clara? There you are," he said. "I trust you found your gift?"

Clara nodded and held up the golden key. "Thank you, Godfather," she said. "Thank you so much."

Drosselmeyer's eye gleamed, a hint of the secret they now shared. "Pin tumbler locks," he mused. "Complicated devils to get into."

"I worked it out," Clara replied happily. "Eventually."

"I knew you would," Drosselmeyer said. He placed a hand upon Clara's shoulder and turned back to the grandfather clock. "Your mother was the cleverest inventor I've ever known. But there was never any doubt when I asked her what her greatest invention was."

"The Realms?" Clara asked.

Drosselmeyer looked down at Clara and smiled. "You," he said.

Clara swelled with pride. She tucked the key safely back into her dress pocket, alongside the precious music box.

"And now," Drosselmeyer said, "I believe there is someone else waiting for you this evening."

Clara followed his gaze to the edge of the room. Her father was standing there, alone, staring sadly at nothing in particular.

She walked over to him and took a deep breath.

"Father?" she asked.

Mr. Stahlbaum turned with a start. "Goodness, Clara, where have you come from? I have been looking all over for you."

"I'm so sorry about the dance," Clara apologized.

Her father patted her arm. "I understand. I wasn't much in the mood for dancing, either."

"Look, I found the key." Clara held up her two treasures: the key and the music box. Her father gently took them and opened the box. Marie's favorite melody tinkled out.

He quickly shut it, pain crossing his face.

"Listen to it," Clara urged him, hopeful. "Don't be sad anymore. She wanted the music to remind us of who she was."

"Full of life," Mr. Stahlbaum reminisced. "And laughter."

"And she wanted it to remind us that we're lucky," Clara said.

"Lucky?" Mr. Stahlbaum asked.

"Yes, Papa," Clara told him. "To have each other."

Emotion still lined her father's face, but his expression lifted.

"Yes, we are very lucky," he agreed.

Clara delicately reopened the music box and placed it on a nearby table. The melody played once more.

"She was telling us that we can dance again." Clara held out her arms. "So, can we?"

Her father thought for a moment, his eyes misty with memory. "Why not, my little mechanic, why not?"

He took Clara in his arms, and together, they danced. Past the Christmas tree, past Fritz and Louise, past the guests and presents and ballroom festivity. Father and daughter, waltzing to their own magical tune playing from a very special tinkerer's treasure, just the way Marie had hoped they would.

Imagination brought to life.